TASTE-TEST YOUR DREAMS.

Don't even try to put that Holy War down. It'll be a losing battle. The #1 song and viral music video by rap sensation Markus is now a TV docuseries, developed by Gen-Z insiders from rising boutique ad agency Pure Creative, in partnership with Telco, the nation's leading mobile service provider. We want to give YOU a taste of
SUCCESS!   FAME! $$$!   HOPE!

HOLY-WAR   IN PARTNERSHIP WITH TELCO®
A NIGHT ARMY | PURE CREATIVE PRODUCTION

The VIRTUOUS ONES

Christopher Stoddard

Christopher Stoddard Copyright © 2022

All rights reserved. No part of this publication may be reproduced, distributed or transmitted in any form or by any means, without prior written permission.

ITNA PRESS
Los Angeles, CA
www.itnapress.com

The author wishes to thank Griffin DeNigris, Bruce Benderson, Darrell Crawford, Daneka Hopper-Okada, Kelsey Liss, and all his friends in advertising.

This is a work of fiction. Names, characters, places, and incidents are a product of the author's imagination. Locales and public names are sometimes used for atmospheric purposes. Any resemblance to actual people, living or dead, or to businesses, companies, events, institutions, or locales is completely coincidental.

Cover photo courtesy of f8archive
Interior photo courtesy of Neil Baylis
Cover & interior artwork by ITNA

The Virtuous Ones by Christopher Stoddard. -- 1st ed.
ISBN 978-0-9976432-0-6
Library of Congress Control Number: 2022935483

For Griffin and the Two-Headed Pigeon

"They are a little like dead people to me, a little like heroes of a novel; they have washed themselves of the sin of existing."
—*Nausea* by Jean-Paul Sartre

CHAPTER ONE

The Heroes

LINK AND THE REST of the Pure team follow Markus's famous DJ and business manager through a maze of dingy hallways with yellowed white walls. The statuesque thirty-something man called Baby is giving them a tour of Madison Square Garden before Markus's show. In the near distance, they hear a restless twenty thousand-plus audience of mostly college men chanting, "Mark-us! Save us! Mark-us! Save us!" Their collective baritone voices reverberate throughout the auditorium and backstage, like the growling belly of a giant beast ravenous for Markus's songs about bedding young women and making mad money.

As part of Markus's entourage for the night, the Pure team is free to roam MSG as if they own the place. Baby took them in via the VIP door. They rode the elevator with a star NBA player, two supermodels, and twin brothers who'd recently won an Oscar for the last film they'd co-directed. As the celebrities chatted up Baby, the Pure team interjected awkward laughs or responded monosyllabically to the few questions addressed to them. They didn't want to blow this one. Even though they've gotten tight with Baby, they know their relationship is strictly business. No time for starfucking when leadership at Pure is pressuring them to lock in Markus and his celebrity friends for such a major advertising campaign as this one.

Link, the creative director of the *Holy War* project team at Pure Creative, a boutique ad agency in SoHo, wasn't turned on by Markus's rap song of the same name until it went viral. That gave him an epiphany. He'd turn the music video for the song into an advertising campaign, but he'd disguise it as a TV docuseries about helping the less fortunate. Being at the top of his game, he knew it'd resonate with Gen-Z, even when a few others at Pure weren't sold. Now look at him, strolling through MSG, planning to save the world with an international idol who has global reach. For once in his career, he doesn't feel like he's contradicting his belief in the importance of truth in advertising. He's also just stoked about doing some real good with one of the most influential entertainers in pop culture today. These months spent developing the series with Baby and his Pure counterparts have been more fulfilling than any of his previous work, even the Nike Air Max campaign for which he was shortlisted at the Cannes Lions Festival of Creativity.

Because of Markus's questionable claim of being half Black and his ruling that any companies he does business with make workplace diversity and inclusion a priority, Pure Creative has tried to put together, quite unsuccessfully, a satisfactory team. Ella, the account director, is a white woman. Executive producer Brandon is a gay white man. The rest are straight white men. Robin is Black, but when Pure promoted her from head of new business to CEO, she had to come off all project work, including *Holy War*, her baby. She couldn't even make the concert tonight because of her busy schedule. As one of the straight white men, Link often feels like an imposter. The others share the sentiment without realizing it, misdiagnosing their shame as performance anxiety. They have yet to meet Markus, and for presentations to the Night Army—his crew—they've been relieving their racing hearts and trembling hands with Ella's prescription of beta blockers. But with the Adderall they chew semi-hourly like Tic Tacs, the stage fright meds offer little relief.

Markus made the music video for his hit song "Holy War" to support underprivileged minorities. It shows him visiting tough neighborhoods in L.A., buying groceries for a full store of shoppers at a Smart & Final, tossing the keys to a shiny new minivan with a bow on it to a waitress walking her five kids three miles to school every day, and slipping a stack of cash to a widower with a tiny newborn in the crook of his arm. Insert Pure Creative to capitalize on the viral music video by developing it into a TV docuseries in partnership with their most lucrative client, Telco. As the largest mobile service provider in the U.S., Telco has asked Pure to create a game-changing ad campaign that will attract millennial subscribers. The most strategic way to do this, Link has advised, is to forgo traditional advertising tropes and instead work with Pure to produce subtly branded content that features relatable celebrity talent.

In the *Holy War* docuseries, Markus and his celebrity friends will go back to the poor neighborhoods of their childhoods to face the crippling opioid crisis and rampant gun violence, and to speak to those affected by the mass incarceration of non-violent drug offenders within the Black community. Each episode will feature local heroes, ending with the guest talent making a charitable donation. Throughout the show, the talent will take calls on Telco's new smartphone, while raving about its premium features and crystal clear connection. Markus will also get to promote his new clothing line via strategic product placement in the show. Any on-camera volunteers will wear black T-shirts printed with "N/A," the Night Army logo, in giant gold letters across the chest, from his spring/summer 2019 collection. A hundred percent of the proceeds will go toward RAINN, the nation's largest anti-sexual violence organization.

An ad agency-produced TV show—the merging of marketing and entertainment like never before—will be unprecedented. If successful, the Pure team on the project and the agency as a whole will become advertising legends. It'll be a win-win-win, with creative awards and industry respect for

Pure, cultural clout and new business for Telco, and money and brand love for Markus.

Backstage, before the concert starts, a stage crew is raising a sparkly helicopter to the ceiling of the auditorium via thin steel ropes—later Link will read it was covered in Swarovski crystals. He's starting to get a little woozy from the surreal, overwhelming scene. His barely eating at a business dinner with the Night Army earlier isn't helping, either. He was too busy schmoozing—plus, it was an Italian restaurant, and he avoids cheese and carbs at all costs. Unlike the rest of the Pure team, he didn't drink during the meeting, nor does he ever. Drugs and alcohol get in the way of him being his best self.

The show finally begins. Everyone on the Pure team is seeing Markus perform live for the first time. The palpable energy he exudes onstage is more impressive than the YouTube videos of previous shows Link has watched. The *Holy War* music video exceeded one billion views this morning, so that may have something to do with it—the track itself has been played three billion times. As the performance continues, they hop from one VIP suite to the next, each filled with celebrities openly smoking weed and snorting lines of various substances.

"No need to pinch yourselves, my friends!" Ella says after the show. As they leave the auditorium, she shows off a thank you text from Baby: "What a vibe tonight, lady. Pure Creative feelin' like fam. Welcome to the Night Army."

Brandon howls into the night.

Link smiles and claps halfheartedly, but the prospect of fame hardly interests him. He's more focused on the charitable element of his materializing vision. His work in advertising was meaningless before *Holy War*, however fruitful financially. He's pumped about making a difference in other people's lives, especially unruly teens in need of guidance. Deep down he still feels like the scrawny kid the bigger boys at Breakneck Military Academy in upstate New York beat up regularly. If only someone had stopped his father from dumping him there after Link's mother had died of breast cancer.

Link's wife, Erica, arrives frazzled but relieved after a late night at her PR firm to share an Uber home with him. A buzzed Brandon and Ella waste no time walking briskly across town, giggly and gossiping as usual, the tall buildings on either side of the street volleying their sassy voices. Link and Erica stay behind to wait for their Uber, arm in arm to keep affectionately warm in the cool night. Minutes and cars pass, but they can still make out the intoxicated pair's manic laughter when they're well out of sight and an avenue away.

At home, in an enviable floor-through apartment on Central Park West—Erica's hedge fund helming father covered the down payment as a wedding gift—she's massaging a few drops of a nighttime serum into Link's forehead as he sips a bedtime tea made with Chaga mushrooms.

"If it wasn't for me, your skin would go to shit."

"I'm nothing without my honeybun," he says, leaning in to kiss her nose as he places the teacup on a marble coffee table. He's wildly horny despite the sleepy time tea, still giddy from his behind-the-scenes experience at the concert. The *Holy War* project is real, his creative ideas are going to make a difference.

They walk into the spacious bedroom holding hands, gazing into each other's loving eyes. Offering up their perfect bodies to one another, they have passionate sex in the vein of actors pretending in a rom-com but with an authenticity that rings truer, something like real love.

Later that night, Ella almost trips on the curb in front of her luxury apartment building. Markus's performance at Madison Square Garden ended hours ago, but she's only just getting home from the bars. Laughing like a hyena at her drunken clumsiness, Brandon catches her by the arm just before she eats concrete. The doorman in the lobby hardly looks up from the video game he's playing on his phone, his reaction to the pair's obnoxious late night arrivals having dulled months ago. They've always been friendly at the office, but after a pleasure trip to Puerto Rico, and with their current collaboration on the *Holy War* project, they've become besties.

In Old San Juan, before flying to Vieques via seaplane, they'd braved La Perla, a poor neighborhood that runs along the coast—the worst place for makeshift homes on a hurricane island. The bartender at La Factoría had told them it was the only place in the city where they could find party supplies, at least as far as he knew.

"Just walk down the stairs by the beach," he'd said flatly.

"How will we find someone?" Brandon had asked.

"They'll see you, they'll come to you."

And come to him they did. While Ella stood back holding her chocolate-and-tan Louis Vuitton handbag like a baby, the locals charged Brandon with plastic kits chock-full of various drugs cradled in their arms. "Coke! Coke! E! E!" the teenage boys shouted in his ears, some shoving bags of coke and weed in one hand while others tried pulling cash from his other, but he held on tightly.

"Everyone back off, back off!" he demanded in the deepest voice he could muster, his entire body shaking.

From a safe distance, one of the taller, older-looking boys tried consoling a hyperventilating Ella. "It's okay, we're not going to hurt you." She nodded but didn't make eye contact as she started to cry.

Brandon believed them. If they robbed all the druggie tourists, the druggie tourists would eventually stop coming with cash, and the locals needed it now more than ever. Hurricane Maria had hit less than a year before. The way he saw it, he was stimulating their economy. Thirty seconds or less later, they had what they wanted and were headed back up the stairs, both feeling like their lives had flashed before their eyes.

Their shared trauma brought them closer. Like honey-mooners, they enjoyed the rest of their stay in Vieques at an elegant hotel called Hix Island House, which had been built on a natural refuge. It was as if the drug dealers in La Perla had murdered them and they were in some heavenly afterlife. Alien-green coqui frogs serenaded their Instagram-scrolling sessions, which evolved into afternoon naps that lasted hours. At sunset, malnourished wild horses deemed pests by the locals decorated the godly secluded beaches that Ella and Brandon drove past on their way to the bars in a rickety jeep rental. A breathtaking tour of the bioluminescent bay, juxta-posed with innumerable stars above them, was more stimulating than any drug-induced experience. They returned to New York with unsightly sunburns, Advil-resistant hang-overs, a Zen-like state of mind, and a friendship that had graduated from superficial to true.

Now that they're back at Ella's place in Brooklyn, the high from the night at Madison Square Garden has lessened from the long commute from Times Square to Williamsburg. She rushes to the liquor cabinet for vodka and cut-off plastic straws.

"Alexa, play 'Possum Kingdom' by Toadies," she orders Echo.

"Oh no, you didn't!"

"Oh yes, I did!"

"I used to love this as a teen."

"Duh, same!"

The place is desperately in need of tidying: dishes piled up, dishwasher full of a clean load from weeks ago, expensive clothes strewn about like disposable fashion, including a rogue pair of Agent Provocateur panties on the kitchen island counter. The bathroom is just as filthy, that is, except for the toilet, which she wipes down every few days with her trusty Clorox Disinfecting Wipes. Soon the mess will overwhelm her, and she'll pop an Adderall and spend hours cleaning, addressing every dirty nook and cranny like a maid on meth. Despite succeeding in becoming a better woman in many ways than her awful alcoholic mother, Ella recognizes she's failed in the housekeeping department. She's been meaning to hire that housecleaner Brandon recommended, but work has been hectic, so she hasn't gotten around to it.

They snort lines off her fancy coffee table and crawl provocatively on the floor to the tune of the Toadies song about a killer who roams around a Texas lake searching for victims. They belt the climactic lyrics at the end of the track with as much lung capacity as they can muster after a night of booze, coke and Capri cigarettes.

The intercom rings in unison with the front door opening to reveal her British boyfriend, Ian. Clearly drunk himself, he stumbles inside and answers the doorman's call.

"Yeah."

"Hi, sir, we've received a complaint about the noise. Can you please turn down the music?"

"All right, mate," he slurs, pushing the red button on the intercom to end the call. In a drunken-zombie stupor from a work function at the members-only club Ludlow House, he half waves at Ella and Brandon on the floor, then beelines for the bedroom and shuts the door.

His ignoring them kills her buzz. "We should wrap it up," she says, trying to control her grinding teeth. "You can stay over, of course."

"No, I better head. Do you have any of those Ambien left?" She fishes a few pills from a drawer in the bathroom—including a couple of Adderall for his looming hungover day at work—and hands them over. "Great night per usual," he says, hugging her goodbye at the front door, which Ian left open.

As he steps into the hallway wide-eyed, five cops in helmets and holding shields nearly run him over. His racing heart is about to escape his chest like he's a Looney Tunes character. "Out of the way!" the cop in front yells.

Brandon takes a step back inside the apartment as the police charge past him. "What's going on?" he asks the last one in line, who's walking slower and not in the same getup.

"Someone called in an attempted suicide." The others bust open someone's door. A woman screams. "Don't worry," the lingering cop cajoles, "this is standard procedure."

But Brandon isn't worried despite his bulged eyes and Ella's nervous disposition as she fidgets behind him. Rather, he's overcome with relief that the cops aren't there to raid her apartment or search his pockets where they'd find the dregs of an eight ball of coke. The memory of their close call in La Perla pops into their minds at the same time. She recalls her younger days in and out of the mental hospital, too, but she keeps that to herself. She grabs his hand, looking him in the eyes. Her eyes say she feels blessed for their friendship, the dangerous situations they've survived together, and the work they're doing on the *Holy War* project—the chemical jolt of heavily cut cocaine likely has something to do with it too.

In front of Ella's building, Brandon is smoking while he waits for his Uber. His left hand is in his jeans pocket, clenching and unclenching. Two unattended police vehicles and an ambulance from which two EMTs are unloading a stretcher are parked across the street, their flashing lights likely waking up some of the residents whose apartments face front. He thinks of the repercussions of suicide, how killing oneself affects so many others. It's certainly left an impression on him. The whole police raid thing has turned him off to finding a late-night hookup after Ella's. Looking up at the four a.m. sky, at its blackness turning a dark gray, he releases a great sigh. The uninvited morning is already surfacing, and with it, the dawn of a new workday at Pure Creative.

Back upstairs, Ella is crawling into bed with Ian, on edge from the drugs and the cops. She lies by his side, her toes creeping around, her restless hand on his chest, slowly making its way down to his crotch. She could use a good lay to help her fall asleep, to lose her mind for a few minutes instead of focusing on the police, her PTSD that the raid has dredged up, and the crazy-busy workday ahead. But Ian is fully clothed, snoring away.

She slides off the bed, tiptoeing to the bathroom. In a drawer under the sink, she grabs her vibrator hidden in a box of tampons, but its battery is dead. She borrows AAA batteries from the Fire TV Stick remote in the living room. Back in the bathroom, the door locked, she sits on the edge of the tub and brings the vibrator to herself, closing her eyes. She fantasizes about her dead brother's best friend and what they did together as teens, but it's not getting her going. Ian comes up, but his violent snoring, audible through two closed doors, turns her off, so she regresses to the ex before him who broke her heart. Finally, she lets go of them all to focus on her dead brother, the only man she really wants or needs, and finishes.

CHAPTER TWO

A Woman in Love

IAN ALREADY LEFT for work. Following the Markus concert and her shenanigans afterward, Ella's waking from another micro-nap on the couch this late Friday morning. Throwing her long, straight, disheveled black hair into a lazy ponytail and moseying into the kitchen, she pours herself a lukewarm cup of coffee, cooling it further with a healthy splash of almond milk. Ian makes six cups every day, four to fill his to-go mug and two for her. Holding the cup in her left hand, she sips the drink while perusing Instagram on her phone with her right.

She fingers the profiles of gorgeous male models William McLarnon and Matthew Noszka, and influencers into extreme sports such as Dylan Efron and Jay Alvarrez, wondering if she'd be happier with a man like one of them: otherworldly sexy, superhero strong and Insta-famous.

"I'm still beautiful," she tells herself in the mirror, despite her slatternly reflection. She checks to see if the Botox that's been hiding the mid-thirties wrinkles on her forehead is wearing off. Thankfully, it hasn't yet.

Surely, if she were in some sort of social setting with these guys, she'd catch their eye. She considers the fantasy for a few more seconds, an even mix of the familiar guilt for her superficial adulterous thinking, an always-on ache for what she can't have, and the growing uncertainty of her love for Ian—very good-looking, much younger than her, and great in bed when she's in the mood—shocking her nerves like the freezing Peconic River on Shelter Island in early June, their first vacation as a couple this past summer. They stayed at the very chic Sunset Beach Hotel.

On the kitchen counter lies her work laptop, with which she emailed her boss earlier in the morning to tell her that she's sick and "working from home." After the late night to early morning partying with Brandon, she can't possibly make it into the office. Thank God he moved the director meetings to Monday, she thinks. Next to her laptop is a bunch of bananas spooning each other inside a clear plastic bag with the Chiquita logo. Dressed in perishable goods, Miss Chiquita smiles festively, ready to perform the calypso dance leap. Once vibrant yellow, the fruits' skin is now dull and freckled, foretelling their rot.

Ian's ask via text remains unfulfilled: "Would you do me a big favor and peel the bananas I left on the counter and put them in the freezer?" That way they'll keep for his weekday smoothies, the making of which is an unwelcome wake-up call for Ella prior to one of Amazon Echo's more appealing alarm sounds. That unnerving jackhammer noise of a "Magic" Bullet Blender pureeing assorted fruit, ice and almond milk is anything but enchanting.

Ella's Williamsburg apartment has two bedrooms and two bathrooms. The luxury building boasts amenities such as a state of the art gym with indoor rock climbing, indoor simulated golf, a mini golf course on the roof, a bowling alley, two pools, three hot tubs and various monthly events—the paint-and-sip class was more sip than paint for her. Some of their neighbors have children and dogs, both of which Ian wants someday too. Ella doesn't think of herself as motherly and has never been a big fan of animals. This isn't to say she's a bad person, just selfish, but she finds an odd comfort in her being conscious of it. Not only that, but one of her biggest fears is repeating the lives of her parents. A part of her will always be running from their ghosts, from becoming them.

Lately, she's been struggling with her somewhat lavish, arguably heretical lifestyle, thinking she should be spending her money and time with Ian in healthier ways, or maybe she's just super hungover. Perhaps it's biological. Her birthday is around the corner, as is her body's inability to make babies. Aside from his smoothies and other behaviors that only annoy her because she's constantly irritable from the weekend-binge comedowns, Ian has been kind and understanding of her idiosyncrasies, addictions and neuroses.

Her last long-term lover, Dylan, a TV actor with obscenely sized emerald eyes who was a couple years older and a few zeros richer than her, acted as her obsession du jour, the co-inciding rush like that of coke. But he never showed her truly selfless love in any form. Instead, he embodied a fantasy of what she'd wanted for oh so many years. A big part of her still does, despite her best efforts to suppress her self-destructive desires. Their relationship involved passionate arguments and occasional violence paired with mawkish, superficial making up sessions and frequent interstices of rough sex, binge-partying and chain-smoking. She hasn't spoken to him in almost five years and refuses to follow him on Instagram or check his IMDb page. When she happens upon an ad for his show, *The Brave One,* while clicking through the apps on her Fire TV, she moves on swiftly, forcing him back into the basement of her mind.

Ian, on the other hand, came into her life unexpectedly. Crashing into her as she ran into a bike lane while rushing to the office one sultry afternoon, he offered her the opposite of what her ex-boyfriend Dylan had. She accepted his love be-grudgingly and has been battling against rejecting it ever since. In fact, she's often perplexed by the idea of true love, and whether this newfound calm affection that doesn't dom-inate her world means she's found a lifetime partner or the deficiency in lust means he isn't the one. The therapist she saw in her teens taught her that those with bipolar disorder shouldn't trust their gut, and this has only exasperated her self-doubting as an adult.

She finds herself more preoccupied with the fear of his imminent departure now that she's hungover again, nearing old age, and getting crazier by the nanosecond. Moreover, her name is the one and only on the lease that ties her financially to this time and place. Ian's technically been living with her for just over six months, and he's only here from England temporarily, working at a design firm on a two-year work visa. He can just get up and go anytime. A slice of her, the demon inside, craves this, as it'll allow her to revert to the life of the manic art slut: hard-working by day as a group account director in advertising, partying with a different date every night, creating her lonely paintings during tear-soaked, suicidal in-betweens. But the rest of her is well familiar with how that old song and dance eventually ends. Peeling and slicing Ian's bananas, she prays un-denominationally that she'll be able to sustain her current commitment to him. She stores the mushy fruit in a plastic container and tosses it in the freezer.

He keeps three tabs of acid in an empty dental floss case on the bottom shelf of her gold-painted metal nightstand. Each piece is the size of her closely manicured pinky nail, but the dealer says they're potent. Flashbacks of her goth-girl teens arise whenever Ian tries convincing her to trip with him. While hallucinating, she'd confronted her anger over the deaths of her abusive parents, fallen in love with painting and a man for the first time, and realized her last best friend—

before her new BFF, Brandon—was anything but, swiftly thereafter ending their toxic relationship. Before her brother Frank died, when Ella was just fifteen, he'd turned her on to acid, believing it'd help her recover from her grief. She fears an LSD-laced epiphany about the future of her relationship with Ian, that it's not destined for married status. But the intensifying self-reflection that goes along with her aging is prompting her to take the acid and find out the truth once and for all.

She rises early the following sun-drenched Saturday morning, slipping softly out of bed to avoid rousing her lover, who spent the second night in a row with old college mates visiting from England, drinking with them till the wee hours of the a.m. He's likely recovering from another hangover anyway, so she doubts he'll be woken up easily. These circumstances are usually flipped. Traditionally, she's the one sleeping off a night of indiscretions while he's already up and at 'em, starting the day right with a smoothie and a three-mile run back and forth over the Williamsburg Bridge, then gently nudging her conscious at about three p.m. with three Advil, a tall glass of ice water and no questions asked. Granted, her last time out was two days ago. But he's been gradually assuming her behavior. It seems the end has begun, and she needs to act now to ensure their best possible future, together or otherwise.

The overly ripe bananas that she put in the freezer for him yesterday are rock hard when she pulls them from their cryo-slumber along with a bag of frozen berries. She places them on a crowded coffee-stained kitchen counter, a collection of half-eaten takeout and countless empty bottles of beer and wine dominating its marble surface. Shaking a near-empty gallon of refrigerated almond milk, she's pleased there's enough left for two smoothies. She tosses everything into a blender cup and switches on the annoying machine.

As she pours the mixture into two glasses and tops off each with a tab and a half of the LSD, she hears rustling sheets, snorting, mumbling and the creaking bed. The door to the bedroom creeps open. Ian emerges yawning and naked, his pale non-gym body exposed and brown hair messy.

"Hey, hon," he says in a raspy voice. "Whoa, you made us breakfast! Thanks, sexy. Just what I needed." He gives her an alcohol-and-rotten-fish-scented kiss on the cheek. She worries that it's another girl she smells but quickly shakes off the thought. Stirring each glass with a bent spoon—they're in dire need of new silverware—she mixes in the secret ingredient.

"Yeah, well, I didn't blend the fruit enough," she says, handing over one of the glasses. "Drink up! It'll help with the hangover. Take these Advil, too." He chucks the pills down his throat and chugs the smoothie. A burp, then he's off to the bathroom for a shit.

Quickly slurping down her serving with a stainless-steel straw—plastic ones are hard to come by nowadays, and the cardboard kind give her the chills—she uses her pointer finger to pull out the soggy tabs of paper stuck on the side of the glass. Not that it matters, as she's sure the hallucinogenic chemicals with which they're laced have already mixed with the drink. His aren't visible after he finishes, so he must've swallowed them. She sucks them off her fingers. The only thing left to do is wait, so she flops down on the couch, ignites the good ol' Fire TV Stick and starts the latest episode of *Euphoria*.

The faint sound of a toilet paper roll rattling around the holder means he's finishing his business. Materializing again, he lets out a deep sigh, dragging his body next to her, bringing with him a waft of Febreze and the stench of a hangover shit. He burps again and chuckles.

"There was this absolutely pissed bum at the bar begging everyone for money, so strange," he shares randomly. "Oh, I've been thinking we should go to Portugal…"

The next day, an impressive Sunday sunrise. Life has already moved on from yesterday's trip, but Ella's certain she never will, not completely anyway. Through the blinds in the bedroom, the six a.m. daylight burns her eyes like a vampire's worst nightmare. She desperately needs blackout curtains. Sleep is always brief for her the night after taking LSD. The overwhelming visual effects she experiences while high never disappear when it's time for shut-eye. Instead, they're more intense. For an hour or two before dozing off, still half-conscious till the a.m., she's stuck watching on her eyelids a cartoon of Dante's *Inferno* in the style of characters from *The Simpsons*.

She rises abruptly, unconcerned with rustling sheets or creaking beds. The reason to keep quiet has been eliminated with her relationship. Ian left her yesterday. He didn't take too kindly to her dosing him. At first, he found it arousing, achieving perhaps the biggest erection she'd ever seen him have. He was giggling uncontrollably at the second episode of *Euphoria*, during which Nate—played by Jacob Elordi, Ella's "gorg" celebrity crush—beats a guy to a pulp and rapes him. As the visuals kicked in, so did her libido and the realization of how much she loved Ian, how passionately generous and unconditionally accepting he'd been with her for the last six months. Her bad habits and emotional baggage, the bold selfishness, he'd ignored it all. While he'd looked the other way on countless occasions, she'd been searching for fulfillment in every direction but his. "How insanely mistaken you were," she told herself. Rushing to her knees, she yanked down his sweatpants and devoured him. The howls he made as she orally coaxed him to completion were magnificent.

"Holy shit, hon, oh my god. That was insane. What's going on? Everything is vibrating."

Barely pulling on his sweatpants, he darted for the bathroom and knelt over the toilet to puke. She walked to the sink beside him and rinsed her mouth, checked herself in the mirror and saw the wrinkles in her forehead become white worms, slither off her face and fly away. Feeling beautiful and perfect, she finally divulged she'd dosed him.

"We're on the acid, hon! I put it in our smoothies. I've just been so horrible lately, pushing you away. You know I've been scared to take it because of the revelations I have on it. But it was worth the risk! I now know I love you so much, and I'm so sorry. I'm going to be better to you, to us."

"You did what! Are you kidding me, Ella? You know my parents are arriving today from London for my dad's birthday. What is wrong with you?"

And just like that... that was that. A few more harsh sentences, including "We're done for good, you crazy cunt!" Packed bags. His snubbing her pleas to refrain from going out in public high or leaving her alone and on drugs. An exit with a slammed front door. Sobbing and hallucinating, she texted him nonstop for hours, but for some reason, she never called. Eventually the blue iMessages turned green, which meant he'd blocked her, shut off his new iPhone or perhaps had even fled the States with his family.

She enters the living room, overcome with sadness and regret. Through swollen eyes underscored with purple bags, she offers a slanting glance at her work computer on a modern glass coffee table with an abstractly shaped oak base, then turns on the TV. She texts Brandon that she's still sick and working from home tomorrow. "Can't I just dial in to the director meetings?"

"Um, the client is in tomorrow. I know you're going through it with your boyfriend or whatever, but you need to get it together. This is your job, Ella. I don't care what you do tonight but be showered and client-ready by eight in the morning."

She knows he's right and that when tomorrow comes, she'll do as she's supposed to, but right now she's in such hideous, paralyzing pain. The last time she felt comparably horrible was during her breakup with Dylan. Prior to that, it had been when her brother had died unexpectedly. Preceding her brother's death had been the violent end of her parents. The years have numbed her a bit, so while her breakup with Ian hurts, the pain is duller.

Ella has replayed in her head her final breakup with Dylan numerous times, attempting in vain to work out what she'd done to deserve such vehement rejection and more loss in her sad life.

"I got the part. I'm moving to L.A. in a week or so," he'd confessed with a joyful, cavalier air. "I don't know the exact date, but the shoot starts in a month, and I need to train for it. They want me ripped."

"But you look great already," she said, always ready to placate his delicate ego, even when he was leaving her.

He went on endlessly, gushing about the call from his agent, how he'd finally made it, and not by luck or networking but on account of his natural talent. A year or so later she'd read an article on *Page Six* about a casting couch situation between him and the series creator, who was rumored to be the gay Harvey Weinstein. In her opinion, Dylan's story was a total cliché, but she'd remained silent as he rambled on. He was too busy talking at her to notice her deadening expression. She may as well have been an inanimate object. The cherry on top of landing the lead role on the new HBO series was an honest excuse to escape his pathetic girlfriend for good. He no longer needed her relentless worshipping of him in and out of the bedroom, which for a time had eased the disappointment of the many rejections he'd gotten when auditioning badly.

From his iPhone he replayed his winning audition video for *The Brave One*, which she'd recorded while reading the lines of the other character off-camera. In his familiarly pretentious tone, he voiced over it like a making-of clip, in between snorting coke and doing pushups on her hardwood floor. Ella absorbed everything miserably. She did a few lines too, while staring dumbly at the dust bunnies he was blowing around the room with each exaggerated exhale he made on the floor. Increasingly distressed, she bit off chunks of skin around her fingernails, causing the tip of her thumb to bleed. The blood looked black in the dim light of the shitty old apartment she'd lived in at the time. He kept talking. His story had an underlying animosity, which was largely directed at her: his repeating the need to rush off with no time for goodbyes and no mention of his feelings about leaving her for a six-month shoot on the other side of the country.

She looked at him with angry desperation as he took a break from his workout to suck up three more lines. He had the perfect excuse to abandon her. The disgustingly cocky insensitivity in the conveyance of his new success, the self-congratulatory way in which he chattered on about how he'd won the part, made her wish she'd had the power to dump him a year before, when he'd first become physically and mentally abusive. She just wanted to run out without another word. Instead of making a move for the door, she crossed the room to the kitchen island, next to where he sat on one of her thrift store barstools—which she's since swapped for expensive home goods now that she's making real money—and fixed herself another line of coke.

Lifting her head from the table, her nose freshly powdered and runny, she opened her painted mouth to say, "So I guess that's it for us? After almost two years? I'll never see you again."

"Us?" he repeated. "What us? I mean, obviously we've been fucking for quite a while, but let's be real. We've been using each other. I'll find others on the West Coast, and you probably will here too... eventually, anyway. It's time to move on."

"And I can move on to hell for all you care, right?"

He smiled in a patronizing and spiteful way. "Baby, what do you want from me? Do you honestly think things would've ended up any other way? My time in New York has been a kind of purgatory. You know I'm a free spirit, not a charity for a lonely girl who chose to get involved with me. That was your choice. And don't give me any crap about how much you did to support me and my career. You wouldn't have done any of it if you weren't getting your kicks out of it, too, even if it was masochistic."

He stood up and pulled down his faded black jeans and his gray Calvin Klein boxer briefs. Ella examined his statuesque physique, her eyes astutely familiar with every inch of him. His enlarging penis, illuminated by the lamp on a side table by the couch, offered a dramatic shadow puppet show on the white wall near the kitchen. He swung both arms behind his beautiful head.

"For old times' sake?" he asked boyishly, as if his horrible words had never been uttered.

"No, I'm done. I'm so done," she said, her eyes brimming with tears.

"The hell you are," he said as he charged at her, laughing hysterically. He grabbed hold of her wrists and forced her to her knees.

"No. No!"

Eventually she gave in. Like all the other times he'd forced her to give him what he'd wanted when she hadn't been willing, she wasn't sure if the whole argument leading up to the sex, their final fuck, was actually nonconsensual or just fore-play. A visceral part of her wanted it, loved it... and him. Later, she shuddered in absolute shame and disgust at the thought of it. Dwelling on it didn't make a difference. She'd never see him again, and that hurt more than anything.

CHAPTER THREE

The Pure Prince

ANOTHER ROMANTIC MONDAY morning in a lovely floor-through apartment on Central Park West. The day greets Link with sunshine floating through massive windows and his wife Erica's sweet morning-breath kisses adorning his torso. Her beige eyes are mere slits as she looks up, smiling her beautiful smile. Amazon Echo continues nudging them with a gentle alarm.

"Alexa off," he instructs, promptly halting its sound. Shutting up is one of the few requests that the not-so-intelligent machine he somehow can't live without knows how to fulfill.

The wet snout of their aging dog, Miley—originally Erica's parents' dog that they left to her before her father partially retired and they moved to Florence—appears on the mattress near her pillow, preventing the body kisses from going lower.

"I'll take the old man out, hon," Link, with a semi-erection, concedes.

Cheerfully, he hops out of bed. She decides to snooze another thirty minutes while he tends to the dog and showers.

The water pressure in their home is perfect, the temperature adjustable to any desirable degree of hot or cold. The stall in the master bathroom is large enough to fit four people comfortably. Link and Erica like to flirt with the idea of inviting others to wash with them. Such dirty talk often precedes a wet fuck, which is as far as they'll ever take their fantasy. They are truly, deeply, in love.

As the soothing water falls from the rain shower head above him, he remembers last night's weird dream about his thieving friends from military school. The students, including Link, committed their childhood crimes through no fault of their own other than growing up with distant asshole parents. Later in life, when they were all too old to blame their bad behavior on the cards they'd been dealt at birth, a couple of them kept breaking the law, more violently then, and are in prison now. Another one overdosed last year. Link isn't surprised. For all of Breakneck Military Academy's unfulfilled promises on their website of outputting great men via their tough love program, they've done nothing but prime juvenile delinquents for a life of incarceration.

In the dream he had last night, a blood red haze was suspended in the air. Ghosts of his past floated in and out of the sequence, trying to instigate emotion, but he felt nothing. The childhood trauma of a verbally abusive father and physically abusive military school has receded over the years with the propulsion of his career and fairytale marriage. Despite all his father's faults, Link, in a way, still loves him. But he'll never forgive him for sending him away shortly after his mother died.

Casually dressed, with a clean-cut smile, short, subtly styled walnut hair and fresh-smelling deodorant, Link bends to wake his wife gently. "You were talking in your sleep again, hon."

"What did I say?" she yawns.

"Something about Instagram, as usual... Dog's walked and fed." He kisses her pillowy lips. "I love you so much."

"Love you, too," she says, stretching thin, toned arms in the air as the shaggy old dog licks her face.

Link offers a polite nod to the Uber driver when she says his name to confirm she's picked up the right passenger. She does so with an extra question mark in her tone. Many do when they first hear his name. When Link and Erica first met, she'd told him he had the same name as a character in a British novel by the late author Anna Kavan, whom she'd read as an English major at Princeton. He has limited memories of his mother, who died of cancer when he was eleven, but he knows she was a British ex-pat and failed actress turned trophy wife. Perhaps she loved Anna Kavan too. He could ask his father, that is, if his father was at all willing to talk about his mother. Link, forever a romantic, saw it as a sign that Erica was his soulmate. She knew him better than he knew himself.

Shutting the car door, he cracks open the window, allowing the cool breeze of fall to tousle his styled brown hair. Bright natural light appears between branches of sun-colored leaves, clarifying his reflection in the glass. In the shadows of the tree-lined street, his face fades again. Instrumental music, something with chimes, plays peacefully at low volume from the backseat speakers. A vent-clip air freshener fills his nose with the relaxing scent of lavender. The serene experience that the driver has created also includes cruising down Central Park West at a sloth's speed, which wouldn't be an issue if Link didn't have an all-staff meeting at nine. Robin, Pure's CEO, is introducing to the agency the new chief creative officer, who's also Link's new boss.

"Do you mind driving a little faster? I'm in a rush."

"Don't worry, my friend," the driver says, gifting the rearview mirror with large, happy eyes. She has an aquiline nose, dramatic upper eyelashes, much shorter lower ones, and unruly black curls spilling out of a neon yellow cap. She stops at the light before it turns red.

To Link's right, two construction workers are pouring concrete for a new sidewalk in front of one of the luxury buildings built in the late 1800s that's been undergoing extreme renovations for months. To his left, a white-haired lady with Slavic features is being walked by her yapping chihuahua. She's smiling at a conventionally attractive, pale-faced man dressed for the trading floor. He's unlocking a Citi Bike and doesn't notice her. A honking horn from the car behind them prompts the driver to step on it.

Satisfied with the accelerated speed, Link relaxes a bit, turning to his iPhone to check work emails. Most of them are meeting invites from Brandon for today's introductory chats with prospective documentary directors for *Holy War*. A semi-late night is inevitable, but work doesn't feel like work when he's living the dream.

Pure Creative's office in SoHo has open seating without assigned desks. Every morning, employees grab the first available spot, plug in, power up and get to work. The daily output of the agency includes endless emails, clever concepts and meticulously designed pitches backed by strategic rationale and data mined from platforms such as Brandwatch and Mintel. Pitches are followed by account leads with pretty faces treating potential clients to forty-dollar cocktails at the latest hotspot in town. Before *Holy War*, Link considered succeeding in advertising to be nothing more than having a knack for manipulating brands and consumers alike into spending money. That's all about to change.

When there isn't an all-agency meeting like today, the staff strolls in anywhere from nine to eleven, depending on their level of seniority. The more senior you are, the later you sleep. A handful of creatives called in earlier this morning, claiming to be sick with a cold, but they're likely just hungover. Link knows there was a birthday party last night for one of the junior designers to which he hadn't been invited. Ever since his promotion, he's received fewer offers from his co-workers to socialize outside of work. Others are traveling on company business or taking advantage of Pure's unlimited vacation policy with their fourth or fifth holiday, while he and a few dedicated others spent the previous weekend working on the *Holy War* project.

When Link enters the large conference room for the all-agency meeting, Ella and Brandon are discussing Axel, Pure's newly appointed chief creative officer, who's channeling Rizzo the Rat from *The Muppets*: hairy misshapen body dressed in a crumpled black T-shirt and wrinkled chinos, frowzy beard and a touch of rot in the corners of a corrupt smile. Some equate his bad hygiene with his European origins.

"As if that's an excuse," Ella snarks.

"If I were European and heard that, I'd be deeply appalled," Brandon replies.

"Um, yeah." She's half listening as she taps a furious reply to a work-related email on her phone.

Link is doing his best to tune out the two of them shitting on his new boss, but they're in the row directly behind him. He's never judged anyone based on looks alone. Besides, the ad rags have lauded Axel's work several times, and he's won more Cannes Lions than two men can comfortably carry.

"I heard he takes credit for his team's work," Brandon continues, as if he were reading Link's thoughts. "No one wins that much."

"Dude, the leg."

Brandon adjusts his impatient leg, so it isn't tapping the bench that Link is sitting on, knowing how much his restlessness irks him. His tone also tells Brandon he's sick of their gossiping, so he shifts the conversation to celebrity news. They've all been working together for almost four years now and know parts of each other better than their significant others do—for better or worse.

As compassionate and unconcerned with superficialities as Link may be, he has the face and body of a Greek god. He stays in shape to maintain his health: his physicality, of course, but his state of mind too. And even though his Erica makes every supermodel look like the girl next door, he fell in love with her mostly because of the unconditional love she gives him. They met in Cabo during a shoot for a Flamin' Hot Cheetos commercial several years ago—Pure was the ad agency, Erica's PR firm the talent management—and honeymooned there last year.

The roughly two hundred employees that make up Pure Creative, including Link, are crowded on hard wooden benches on the floor of an auditorium-sized conference room—the agency calls the space Shakespeare and often leases it out for various performances and speaking engagements. The leadership team and some senior level employees relax on cushioned seats in the loft above them, but Link prefers to stay with the larger team. He was only just promoted to creative director a couple of months ago.

"Did someone order a legend?" Axel proclaims, sliding onstage like a black-and-white Dracula through dry ice.

Perhaps it's his sophisticated accent that commands hearty laughter and applause from the lot of them. Link chuckles and claps but wonders if the guy is serious. He can almost sense Ella and Brandon rolling their eyes behind him. Remembering Axel was a locally famous standup comedian in Sweden, Link assumes—hopes—that he's joking.

Pure's CEO Robin, the sole Black person and woman in a leadership role at the agency, follows a fiery Axel onstage. Her arms relax at her sides with a wireless microphone in her right hand. She offered it to Axel before he went on. He snubbed it, boasting that his public speaking voice carried naturally. As would anyone's when screaming like a maniac, she thinks, as she's waving at the staff.

Axel tells another self-serving joke. His bravado aside, she's thrilled to have him join the team. They've been craving a new leader to take the creative reins for months. Finding someone specialized enough for Pure's diverse portfolio of clients proved to be a monumental challenge. The agency has garnered a strong reputation for transcending the concept of non-traditional advertising into something like art for the future, so they had to choose their new chief creative officer wisely.

Their former CCO was regarded as a messiah in his own right, at least until allegations of sexual assault decorated the front of *The New York Times* on the day before Christmas Eve. Robin's predecessor was also called out in the article and fired just the same. She'd been caught by surprise when the board of Pure's holding company had requested a meeting with her two days before the story broke.

"There's going to be an article coming out on Friday, and we're preparing a response. Your CEO will be stepping down tomorrow, and we want you to take his place. Your dedication and passion for the growth of this agency hasn't gone unnoticed."

Prior to the offer, Robin had been heading the strategy and new business departments—Pure is a small agency, so employees wear many hats. She'd loved her job then, had been proud of the rapport she'd built with their clients, and how, with her cross-industry expertise in marketing strategy and inimitable relationship-building skills, she'd made the young agency a profitable business.

Despite being a department head, she embedded herself in high profile project work. She was especially invested in the *Holy War* project because she'd been the catalyst for bringing it to life. She'd already consulted on the brand launch for Markus's DJ and business manager Baby's marijuana dispensary in L.A., which has since become a profitable chain in Southern California. When Link and team had come up with the great idea of turning the *Holy War* music video into a TV docuseries, all she had had to do was text Baby and a meeting had been set.

She knew that if she accepted Leadership's offer of CEO, she'd have had no more time to work on projects, which might've been problematic for *Holy War* since she'd been the only person of color working on it, and diversity is mandatory for all of Markus's dealings. But the rest of the Pure team on *Holy War* had developed a trust with his crew, the Night Army, despite being white. She ultimately took the offer, realizing it was time to let go, that with talent like theirs she *could* let go, allowing her to invest her energy influencing the rest of the agency to operate and create as seamlessly and originally as they had.

"I. Am. Your. New. Cult. Leader!" Axel declares.

The staff screams in appreciation, especially the creatives who've been starved for direction since the last CCO's demise. Axel does a little Adderall-charged dance around the stage.

"What a copycat cunt," Brandon whispers loudly. "To say Axel's behavior mirrors the charming manic quirks of his predecessor is the understatement of the new century."

"For almost four years," Axel continues, pacing the stage, "Pure Creative has used the individuality of your souls, the mind's eye inside *each and every one of you* to purify our clients' brands. We tell true stories, never false claims. We bring excitement to the facts, never glazing over them with bullshit. Because brands should level with their consumers, genuinely connect with them and their needs, and never manipulate them. We keep it real. And when we go to sleep each night after another long, passionate day of creating pure advertising, we rest easy, satisfied and proud. We. Are. Pure!"

Link scans the room, which Axel's words have blanketed in silence like a snowstorm in the city. Even Ella and Brandon have stopped their gossiping. Brandon breaks the quiet with an obnoxiously loud, ironic cheer. The rest of the agency follows suit. Axel nods and wipes his nose, waving his hand in the air, signaling for them to simmer down so he can continue.

"With a presence in thirty-eight countries," he says, coughing, "we've reimagined the household brands of this planet, and we're just beginning. *You* are just beginning."

The black curtain draped over the twenty-foot wall behind him rises with his words, revealing a hand-painted mural of Pure Creative's new branding, which he designed. The agency's manifesto is written in black and sky-blue graffiti, the words virtually identical to his speech. Nestled in the center of the wall of words is an illustration of a Black baby girl with one feathered white wing of an angel, the other a bald and bony demon's wing. The baby is emerging from an abstractly shaped vagina. From both sides of the stage two tattooists appear, their illustrated arms holding stick-and-poke kits.

"My new Pure family, I invite you all to join me in the most authentic branding known to man: stick-and-poke tattoos. Let the separation of your body and Pure art disappear. Look to the new mantra of our lives, *your* lives," Axel says gesturing to the wall. "Choose any word or image and literally *etch* it into your body. *I* am your *fucking* body! *We* are your brand! We are *everybody*! We! Are! Pure!"

And the crowd goes wild.

"Team, team, settle down a moment," Robin says gently, raising a hand. The left sleeve of her flowy A.L.C. dress in a bold diamond print falls to her elbow. Her kind, soulful voice works like a charm: the audience quiets again. With fidgety hands, Axel stands by as idly as possible.

"While everyone is welcome to get a tattoo to honor the agency and our new branding," she continues, "please know it's not mandatory. There are other ways to represent the sentiments of Pure, and that is through your work, your creativity. Creativity comes from all departments, not just the creative team. Brave, cross-departmental ideas and collaboration are why we are Pure and why this beautiful artwork is a true symbol of us. The shining example of this is the *Holy War* project. Can the beautiful humans working on it please stand if you're not already?"

Link rises, nodding modestly. He checks the time on his Apple Watch discreetly, concerned that they'll be late for their meetings with the directors. Ella, Brandon and the support staff working under them are already on their feet, amusing everyone with Miss America waves.

"As everyone knows," Robin says, "I personally invested my heart and time in the *Holy War* project because of what it represents: branded entertainment that helps people rather than just selling to them. It couldn't have been done without the expertise of everyone standing: creative, client service, strategy and production. Together, we make beautiful things happen by finding new ways for brands to matter to the world via authentic, entertainment-focused content that touches souls and leaves a permanent impression on them. Many thanks and big hugs to all of you!"

The employees respond with genuine applause, but their sentimental moment is short-lived. Axel, in a subconscious effort to redirect their attention to him, plays "Sex with Me" by Rihanna from the speaker system at deafening volume. The office manager and receptionist roll out tables of mimosas and trays of hot breakfast foods. The tattooists unfold metal chairs onstage. Axel rocks his anorexia-inspired hips to the music as he exits the room in haste, desperate for a cigarette—he smokes two packs a day.

Robin steps offstage with Link's help, joining the agency on the main floor of the room. Walking slowly down the aisle between the benches, she hugs and shakes hands with the staff still in their seats, as others are forming a long line to get tattoos.

"I love your dress," Ella says after she and Robin make kiss noises by each other's cheeks.

"Thank you, Ella. I always appreciate your taste."

"Aw, thank you, Robin. You have the best style."

As Robin passes, she whispers in her ear, "It's from Rent the Runway."

"Oh, I'll never tell," Ella replies, a touch condescendingly.

The rest of the day at Pure progresses in expectedly manic, challenging fashion. Link has rejected every director they've met other than the one Axel scared away in the morning. The director in-mention had been nominated for an Oscar for best documentary feature three years ago: a film about the hottest day of summer in crime-ridden Chicago, during which gang violence is statistically at its peak. Ella, Brandon, Link and two mid-level creatives on his team were engaged in a stimulating conversation about the subject and Link's overall creative vision for *Holy War* when Axel barged in to offer his two cents.

"Gangs etcetera in the inner city is a strong topic, sure, but for *Holy War* to be successful, the focus can't just be on the ghetto boys of America. We can do better."

The director, who'd said in several interviews that he's from the world he'd documented, immediately terminated the meeting and called his agent, understandably furious. Other than Axel, everyone blushed and tensed.

Link didn't want to call out his new boss in front of the group, so he asked him for a quick sidebar just outside the conference room. "I know you're new to this project, man, and we're all stoked you're here," he said. "I'm all for pushing the work, but we've been developing this show for over a year and are more familiar with the sensitivities of the subject matter and how to speak to the talent. We're charting new territory here. This isn't a straight ad campaign. These are real people and stories, and we're building a team to help tell them."

"What, what'd I say?" Axel asked.

A visibly stressed Brandon ran past them with angry eyes to smooth things over with his contacts at Creative Artists Agency.

"If this gets back to Markus or the client, this project is as good as canceled," a hungover Ella interjected from her seat in the conference room, obviously eavesdropping.

She texted Robin about what had happened. Robin, in turn, had a long, diplomatic chat with Axel, suggesting he sit out the rest of the director meetings for the week because he hadn't been fully onboarded yet. He agreed, but the circumstances left a bad taste in his mouth. Such babies, he thought, while on his fifth cigarette break of the day.

"We'll keep looking, guys. This lot just wasn't meant to be," Link says, pep talking the defeated *Holy War* team at the end of the day.

"I guess you're right," Brandon agrees, rubbing ointment over a fresh stick-and-poke tattoo of a demon's wing on his right wrist. "CAA is sending me more names by morning."

Link's evening is like any other weeknight: a frantic rush to a CrossFit class a few blocks from the office. He squeezes into a tight spot in the corner of the studio, disregarding one or two eye-rolls for arriving late. Struggling to focus, he's distracted by a new chain of emails about Telco's feedback on the storyboards for the pilot episode of *Holy War*. There isn't enough brand integration. Apparently, credits in the title card and having the talent use Telco's phones on camera aren't enough for them. Telco is suggesting culturally suicidal ideas such as Telco-branded T-shirts worn by the celebrity guests in each episode—in addition to the on camera volunteers already having to wear tops from Markus's clothing line. Their antiquated marketing team doesn't understand the concept of subtle branding. If they want *Holy War* to rival other docuseries to which they're aspiring, particularly *The Defiant Ones* for Beats by Dr. Dre, they'll need to acquiesce to Pure's expert recommendations.

Erica texts Link two kiss-blowing smiley faces and four red heart emojis, asking him what time he'll be home for dinner because it's getting late. Then he realizes he forgot to return a pair of ill-fitting pants to the Saturdays store by the office. Their exchange policy for his purchase expires today.

"Class can't begin till all phones are put away!" There's nothing passive aggressive about the CrossFit instructor's order. He's staring down at Link from the front of the room.

A few others are looking back too, more visibly annoyed than when he showed up in the middle of the warm-up. A woman who hit on him at his former job, knowing he was already taken, is two rows up and three athletes to the left. She doesn't immediately recognize him or is pretending she doesn't.

After class, his sweat-soaked skin meets fifty-five degree air outside. Hailing a cab home is surprisingly easy. Passing car lights smear in front of his eyes like electric paint in the air. Time to swap out his disposable contacts for a fresh pair. Flashbacks of exhilarating nights cloud his vision, such as the times he snuck out of the boarding school to hit nightclubs in the city, where he watched as his underage classmates got wasted. Guilty longing for his younger years when his schedule was less predictable quickly dissipates. His defiant behavior as a teen only further strained his relationship with his father, despite his never touching drugs or alcohol like his friends had.

At least he has Erica. She greets him at the elevator that opens directly into their apartment, as lovingly as she did when they woke up this morning, as if she never left bed or lost anyone or anything, or never met the simple stresses of a long workday, as if life is always as exceptional as it is in this lucky, basic moment. Glass of white wine in one hand, a tumbler of his favorite kombucha in the other, she shows him to his seat at the solid blackwood dining room table. A feast of raw fish from Sushi Yasuda that she ordered all by herself awaits—she's no at-home chef.

"Oh my god, the delivery guy was FaceTiming *in Asian* or something when I answered the door. I had to ask him for a pen to sign at least three times. When he left, I just said konnichi wa! LOL!"

As generous and sweet as Erica is with him and others, giving to charity and all the other things rich people do with their money, she has an aggressive prejudice against Asians, which Link has always found disturbing.

"Honey, that's kind of harsh. You need to be careful these days... What if HR at your PR firm heard a recording of that?"

"Oh, stop, we're in the privacy of our home. It's funny!"

Their old dog Miley materializes from the bedroom, whimpering with elation for Link's return home: their little family together again.

CHAPTER FOUR

Mrs. Diet Coke

ELLA WIPES SUGAR OFF her lap, wrinkling her black mini dress from Vetements. With a half-empty bag of sour gummies on the seat adjacent hers, she hopes to ward off new passengers boarding the busy train. The candy and a Diet Coke are her lunch on this bright Tuesday. It's been a sunny afternoon, but on her way to Grand Central, she noticed dark clouds in the near distance. She runs a hand over her long, straight, black hair, which sits shiny and thick on her petite shoulders. Her eyes examine her lithe porcelain legs with what she deems an impressive thigh gap and her dainty feet in the Eiffel Tower Stilettos also by Vetements.

A mild panic attack may be coming on. Is she too "fashion" for a wake? After all, the viewing is at a funeral home in Stratford, Connecticut, where the white underclass walks a fine line between decent and trashy. As the train pulls out of the station, she catches her reflection in a fingerprint-filthy window, calming slightly at the sight of her perfectly understated face by Glossier: Priming Moisturizer, a touch of Stretch Concealer under her eyes and finished with Future-Dew serum for that dewy-all-day look. She *could* use a little lip. Luckily, she always carries Vice Lipstick by Urban Decay in her purse. It has a sheer, shimmery finish. The dirty pink color is called Ex-Girlfriend. Yes, *yes*, she knows matte is the finish du jour, but she prefers a little extra something. She's a little extra herself.

This is her first wake since her brother died. Open casket, young person, the whole nine. The deceased guest of honor was the son of her brother's best friend, Clay. The son, Bryce, jumped off the Hudson Yards Vessel, the second suicide there this year. Unlike most young Americans dying of opioids these days, drugs weren't the cause. He killed himself over a broken heart. At least that's what everyone assumes because Bryce's girlfriend relocated to California and hadn't asked him to come with her. He'd been devastated and depressed for weeks. The police didn't find a note in his blood-drenched pockets, in his dorm or back home at Clay's.

Ella doesn't understand why they always think it's for one reason. It could've been several or none. He could've been bored. She gets it. She used to fantasize about cutting herself open as a joke on old frenemies and hateful exes, to torture them with eternal guilt for what they made her do, but she's never gone through with it. She wonders if her suicide would affect them long term or if they'd just be a tad sad in the moment, then forget about the whole thing like bad news in yesterday's paper. She wouldn't be alive to see their reaction anyway.

Bryce was a full-time star athlete at UCONN and part-time print model signed with Wilhelmina. The model bit noted in his obituary in the *Connecticut Post* inspired her outfit today. There are sure to be some male models present to pay their respects. Perhaps she'll find love in a dark place.

At the funeral home, the vibe is not at all as expected. The line begins way in the back of the newly tarred parking lot, which glistens with cold rain. She left on the train the umbrella that Brandon had loaned her, and he won't be too happy it's gone. To her left, the floodlights of the funeral home are staring blindingly from the roof, creating a deranged shadow of her drenched body and the mourners proceeding in silence behind and in front of her. She tripped exiting the Uber, and the Eiffel Tower-inspired heel broke off her right shoe, so she had to swap them for the pink Nike trainers in her bag. Their use was formerly restricted to Equinox sessions and the occasional Solidcore or Rumble class. No need to worry about being too "fashion" now, she thinks. The older couple in front of her have been sharing the outer part of their umbrella with her, but the rain is still hitting the back of her head. Her lush hair is going limp. The wet dress is exasperating her need to pee.

Fifteen excruciating minutes later, she makes it to the entrance. An aging usher opens the door, greeting her with a nod. She recalls the lanky teenage boy with tousled brown hair in reflective gear directing traffic in the parking lot and compares him to this guy. Given these businesses are commonly family run, she wonders if they're related and whom else from the funeral home family she'll see along the journey to pay respects to a dead body. The old HBO series *Six Feet Under* comes to mind.

The funeral home family must be so familiar with the myriad ways people of different age groups die, she muses. They can probably assume the size of the turnout based on the deceased's age. Piles of tissue boxes stationed on tables set up along the dreary, twisting line to the casket suggest the family has been expecting a full house, a tsunami of tears to fall from the eyes of Bryce's parents and relatives, his inconsolable hot friends and *their* parents.

"Thanks," she says to the old usher. "Can you please direct me to the restroom?"

"Past where the line curves right for the second time, then make a left. You can take a shortcut through the side door here." His voice is exquisite, perfect for a wake: crystal clear but pillow soft out of respect for the dead. It must've taken years of practice. He opens the side door, revealing a shortcut to the front of the line.

Ella immediately spots Clay hugging one of the mourners. Locking sad, desperate eyes with his, she retreats in a panic. "You know what, I'll just wait."

The usher nods and quickly returns to his post.

Her forehead is no longer just wet from the rain. She's flushed and sweaty from spotting Clay, which ignites the embers of old pain, setting them ablaze, her parents, and her brother Frank, who was Clay's best friend. She clenches her toes so intensely that she's pulling up the soles of her trainers, which will put a damper on her balance in barre class.

Everyone she loves eventually leaves, through death or otherwise. Ian left because she revealed too much of the damaged loon she is. The same goes for Dylan but in a different way. All she has left are co-workers disguised as supposed close friends, yet none of them were willing to come with her, not even Brandon. They're only tight because they have no choice: they're with each other for twelve-hour workdays and a couple weekends a month, toiling away on the *Holy War* project. She scoffs thinking of the motley crew at Pure Creative. They don't give a crap about anyone or anything other than themselves and their careers, and she's no different. She hasn't been doing the work on *Holy War* because she wants to help people. Her goals are consciously self-serving: PR for Pure and a promotion for her.

The sounds of agony are all around her. Sobs, moans and wails reverberate against the suffocating wallpapered walls and low ceiling. She's worried she won't be able to breathe if she stays much longer. The grief in the air is too palpable and overly reminiscent of her own familial losses from which she hasn't fully recovered and probably never will.

The line of mourners is a reptile made of black raincoats and leaky eyes snaking through the funeral home. She arrives at the guestbook, which everyone signs to prove they were there, that they shared in Clay's pain. She scribbles her illegible signature with great pride, believing it'd be *the best* autograph if she were famous. As much as she's suffering through this, she tells herself it's only fair. Clay was there for Frank when his and Ella's parents died, and he was there for her when Frank died. Hell, she lost her virginity to him when she was twelve and he was eighteen—but she'd initiated it. Clay sired Bryce just four years later. She was already off to New York with many promiscuous adventures before her. She's seen him thrice since her teens, this moment included.

The thought comes to mind as she inspects the photos in the collages of Bryce that are positioned sporadically along the path to his dead body. The pics of Clay holding the newborn version of his son, *that's* the man she remembers boning: big, kind eyes, football shoulders, tight torso and a beautiful smile. Looking ahead to Clay greeting the mourners as they reach the casket of the dead version of his son, she strains to recognize the man she once knew. He's much bulkier now. His broad shoulders have become so swollen that she can't see his neck, and he has a bit of a gut. The face is still cute, but his widened head appears squished into the hunk of living meat, aka his body.

Other than him and his wife, to whom Ella's getting dangerously closer, she doesn't recognize anyone or just doesn't remember them. She never even met Bryce. The sad freaks all around her are strangers. Some of them acknowledge her with a nod or talk in low voices with eyes pointed at her. What are they saying? Those fuckers! She curses the rain for ruining her chic look that was more than befitting a runway show or the wake of a childhood friend's son with male model friends. Clay's wife, Kate, stands solemnly by him in a black pantsuit. Her bleached-blond bob is quite unbecoming for such a round face. Ella recalls Clay showing her a picture of his wife when she saw him last, nearly three years ago. He didn't look great then, either, but now... *whoa*. Kate, who was stepmother to Clay's son—the biological mother had allowed full custody to Clay when Bryce was eleven—is noticeably heavier.

Three years ago, Clay invited Ella to Connecticut on the anniversary of Frank's death. They got drunk at her brother's favorite bar, The Salty Dog Saloon in New Haven. She even rode the mechanical bull and won a pitcher of beer and two hundred and fifty dollars for hanging on the longest, which was quite the feat, considering her blood alcohol level. The zigzagging car ride from the bar back to the train station was filled with the reckless laughter of the immortal teens they'd once been. The silly reminiscence turned into flirtatious talk, which she initiated just as she had at twelve.

"Remember that time you banged me in my brother's room?"

He cleared his throat but said nothing.

"Sorry, I hope that wasn't weird to bring up. We just had so much fun back then."

"No, no, not at all, it's okay," he said, pulling the car over. At first she thought he was parking to make a move but then realized they were at the train station. His phone, which was connected to the car's built-in Bluetooth, began ringing from the car speakers. He quickly answered it. "Hey baby," he said louder than necessary, "just dropping Ella at the train. You're on speaker by the way."

"Oh, hi Ella! So sorry we never got to meet, but I had to close and do inventory tonight. My husband isn't drunk driving you home, I hope," said Kate, who managed a craft store then.

Ella hesitated before answering. She looked into Clay's big, kind eyes, which looked heavy from alcohol and had a glint of worry in them for what crazy Ella might say next. Or was it guilt because a part of him wanted her? The truth was irrelevant. Her coital desires wouldn't be sated that night. The realization of this came with a sudden onslaught of grief for her brother on that anniversary of his death. "No, no, we only had a beer. He's totally fine," she lied.

In truth, he was completely inebriated then and looks much worse now. But at least he seems to have a system down for greeting mourners by gender. Men in the general group get a handshake and direct eye contact. Men he's closer to get a handshake, direct eye contact and a pat on the right shoulder. Only in rare instances does he grant a man a full hug, pulling him in and slapping his back. Despite how progressive the world may be, she still believes insecure straight men hugging can be aggressive and awkward. Clay hugs virtually every woman in line. Some instigate further affection, a kiss on the cheek, a shared moment of sobbing, but no more than fifteen seconds, as Ella has timed. Occasionally, a woman will engage him in another fifteen to twenty seconds of conversation about how beautiful Bryce was or to reflect on a happy memory of him.

Paying respects at a wake reminds Ella of the Divine Right of Kings, the belief that God pre-chose the souls who would inhabit the bodies of kings and queens prior to their births. Because of this, royalty is the closest to God one can be on earth. The same can be said for those who've mourned the death of someone as dear as an immediate family member. Like the Divine Right of Kings, death brings one closer to godly. They've experienced up close the hand—the wrath—of God. Clay, His Royal Majesty, stands at the front of the room. His mother, Her Royal Majesty, and Kate, Her Royal Highness, are beside him in silent solemnity. Their people wait in an endless line to kiss the hands of God.

Ella finally reaches Clay just as he's finishing up a level two man-hug. She's convinced he saw her in his periphery and isn't acknowledging her any sooner than he has to. His head seems further embedded in his shoulders. Slap some green body paint on him, and he's a Teenage Mutant Ninja Turtle, she thinks, but the hot one, Raphael. She touches his shoulder lightly as he's nodding goodbye to the old man in line before her, and it startles him. She's broken the system.

"Hi," she says softly, her wet, wilted hair, pale face and ruined makeup giving her Samara-from-*The-Ring* vibes. She clenches her thighs as tightly as possible to avoid pissing herself. This damn impressive thigh gap, she thinks.

"Ella, thank you for coming," he says in the voice of a zombie, his red-ringed, puffy eyes devoid of a soul. She sees nothing divine in him.

He extends a hand, which shocks her. Ignoring the impersonal gesture, she wraps her arms around him. For a split second he doesn't move but quickly gives in. His giant body falls limp in her skinny frame and emits an inhuman wail. She uses her legs to hold the two-hundred-plus-pound muscleman, with the strength she's gained from all those Best Butt Ever classes at Equinox.

"Ella! He's gone! My baby is gone. Oh God, why did He take them from us." By "them" she knows he means his son Bryce and her brother Frank. Both deaths have taken their toll.

"I know, I know. I'm here. I know," she says, her bottom lip quivering, her entire body vibrating with his pain and her anxiety. "I won't cry, I won't fucking cry," she mouths silently. But the tears are coming like a furious tsunami. The pain needs out. Just as her eyes are about to erupt, she slams them shut tighter than a little girl hiding from the boogeyman. She can't let it out.

"Ella... Um, hey Ella."

Clay has pulled away from her to reveal a wet, dark yellow stain on his light gray suit pants. He's looking down at her lithe porcelain legs, as are others around them, including his mother who's aging beautifully and whom Ella hasn't seen since she was a teenager, and Kate, whose round face is cold and hardened like that of a dead baby. Ella smells it before she feels it. The room has gone completely silent. All moist eyes are on her, a skinny, underdressed, bedraggled bitch pissing herself. A small yellow puddle is forming around her trainers on the bright white carpet. Without so much as a glance at Bryce in his casket or another comforting word to Clay, she leaves the room. In her mind she's running, but in reality her body is moving at a snail's pace. Still, no one follows her.

"Is your purse real Louis Vuitton?" Clay asks Ella outside the Mexican restaurant where they've just had a liquid lunch, a couple weeks after the wake.

She's impressed that he recognizes the designer, even one as widely known as Louis. He's never been very stylish. His clothes have an Old Navy wash-and-wear look. She's still oddly attracted to him, though. "Yep!" She giggles like a shy schoolgirl.

"Look at you!" His peppy, almost flirtatious tone is surprising, considering how morose he was when he collected her from the train station. Must be the tequila, she surmises.

"Yeah, L.V. is making a comeback with younger people now that Virgil Abloh is at the helm... although he only does their men's line, and not that I'm exactly *young*."

"Virgil Ab-who?"

Tired of talking fashion with a simple suburban dude like him, she changes the subject to something she was too uncomfortable to bring up earlier. "So, I know we've been having a great time today. I don't want to make this awkward and thank you for not bringing it up because it was *the most* embarrassing moment of my entire existence, but I'm sorry about the... incident... at the wake. I had a long train ride and was overwhelmed by the whole thing. That never happens and—"

"Don't worry about it. You're human. Did I ever tell you about the time I shit my pants?"

"Um, no, what the hell? Sorry, that's so funny. I was *not* expecting you to say that."

"Yup. I was sloshed, and my stomach was all kinds of fucked. I was in shorts, and Bryce caught me coming into the house with diarrhea running down my legs. He never let me forget it. He was like ten or eleven then? Whenever I lecture him about something, he just says at least he didn't take a dump in his shorts. Nine times out of ten that puts me in my place."

The bittersweet memory is a black cloud forming over his head. He's remembering for the umpteenth time that Bryce will never joke with him, nor anyone else, ever again. Ella lays her left arm across his shoulders, pulling him toward her. In this potholed parking lot, behind the Mexican restaurant by the Stratford train station—their teen haunt—he whimpers in her mosquito-bite-sized boobs. She knew that alone time with Clay, without the morbid backdrop of his son's corpse and the uncomfortable looks from his oblivious wife, would be the only way to redeem herself as his eternal temptress. By reconnecting with Ella, the sister of his dead best friend, he can relive the bromance and bang her too.

For days after her piss-poor performance at the wake, she was completely wrecked. She couldn't work or sleep, and she cried every time she peed. Eventually pulling herself together, as she always has and forever will as a tough survivalist, she devised this plan to see him again and set things right. Comforted in their full-body hug, he pulls away with a semi-erection, unlocking his filthy old black Mustang, which was brand new when they reunited nearly three years ago. They hop in.

She never expected these would be the circumstances under which they'd be seeing each other again, although death hasn't shocked her for years. By now she's memorized the templated words of comfort to spit out like she does the lyrics to every Fiona Apple song ever recorded—she's *obsessed*—as well as the socially acceptable expressions one must exercise when first hearing the oh-so-tragic news, attending the wake or the funeral, and during the one or two obligatory pity-hangs post-burial with the bereaved. Behind the scenes she's numb. Everyone dies, she thinks. The whole he-had-his-whole-life-ahead-of-him sob story is such a cliché. The only difference between croaking young and dying old is your adjectives: pretty with potential or wrinkled with regret. At least Bryce looked hot in his casket.

Clay hands her another Newport, her third in two hours. Already full of menthol smokes and countless shots of tequila, she accepts it reluctantly. She wasn't in the mood to eat anything that the train-stop Mexican restaurant had to offer, so her empty stomach has fueled her intoxication. Enchiladas and quesadillas may have been fine as a teen, but now she's a woman in her thirties with a hot figure to maintain.

Admittedly, Ella was famished on the train ride up earlier. She hadn't eaten before or after partaking in back-to-back classes at Equinox, which had included a high-intensity interval-training workout and a so-so challenging cycling class—her weekend routine on the rare occasion she isn't hungover—but her appetite disappeared when she stepped off the train at the Stratford stop. She found Clay smoking in his car, hunched in a way that spoke volumes about how much he hadn't wanted to have lunch with anyone, let alone her. Visiting her hometown always comes with bad memories and all the wrong feelings, but she felt double-triple worse than usual.

Despite the dire circumstances, she was determined to make their time together a success. If he wanted to talk about his kid, she'd listen, but she wouldn't be the one to broach the topic. After the liquid icebreakers, they had a few laughs rekindling their younger years with her brother, like the time they'd stolen two forty-ounce bottles of Olde English from the corner store and had been caught red-handed. Lucky for them, the clerk hadn't called the cops. Completely unrelated to the subject, Clay handed her his phone with the eulogy he'd read for a packed church. Then came the last text message exchange he and his son had ever had.

"U good, how's school, bud?"

"Yeah dad. Love you."

Clay told her he hadn't seen Bryce in a month because he'd been in inpatient rehab for alcoholism, and he'd never forgive himself for his clueless absence. She glanced at the row of empty shots. "Don't worry," he said. "I'm determined not to let this shit take over my life just because I'm going through this."

She felt a little guilty for enabling him but quickly brushed it off—she has her own substance problems to deal with. Showing off the faint red tattoo on her wrist of her brother's initials in cursive, she encouraged him to consider doing something comparable to commemorate his son.

"Oh, I'm planning on it," he said, looking down at his arms tatted up more than a Hell's Angel's. He thumbed through his phone to show her a pic of the son's tattoo on the back of his right hand: Markus's Night Army logo—he'd been Bryce's favorite rapper—a simple lockup of "N/A" in block letters. "I'm getting the same one."

"Wow, that's... huge."

"It's important."

He sounded mildly offended, so she changed the subject to the *Holy War* project, divulging confidential details. "Bryce would've loved this."

After the liquid lunch and chat, staring blankly through the filmy windshield, Clay asks, "Where to next?"

"I should probably get back... I have a seven a.m. client call tomorrow," she lies. "The next train is in twenty or so. We can kill time in the parking lot at the station like back in the day?"

"Cool, cool."

She knows she's not getting any when he's in mourning, and one of her biggest turnoffs is men who cry. But does she really want any anyway? The last time they hooked up, she was pre-pubescent. She just wants her brother back, and Clay is the closest living alternative.

He pulls out of the restaurant's parking lot with a cigarette in his mouth, car windows shut. The one in her hand remains unlit. Making a right around the corner, he turns into the parking lot of the train station. Ella wonders if the rich teens of Darien loitered in as many parking lots in the nineties as she and Clay did in shitty Stratford. He parks near the stairs that lead to the tracks as he increases the volume of the reggae playing from his speakers, which she despises more than country music.

"You should come to mine in the city next time," she says. "We can get drunk or whatever."

"Yeah, maybe."

"Do you ever go to New York?"

"Yeah, I DJ once a month at a club in Queens."

"Oh, fun, I didn't know."

"Just a side thing. Mostly reggae. This is one of my sets we're listening to."

She pretends to listen intently for a second, bobbing her head to the slow beats. "Sounds great. What's your DJ name?"

"DJ Cray Clay."

"OMG stop." He looks hurt, so she follows up with, "You're really good. Would love to see you play live."

"Thanks."

"Okay, I think I'll go wait by the tracks. Don't want to miss it."

"You sure?"

"Totally. I'm glad we had this time. Let's hang again when you're feeling up to it."

"Cool."

She leans her face near his, unsure if she's going in for a kiss on the cheek, mouth or just a hug. He opens his arms for an embrace, resting his chin on her shoulder.

"Thanks for coming. It was great seeing you," he says without inflection.

A gaggle of teenage girls in skater attire are laughing derisively at Ella as she waits on one of the metal benches along the platform next to the tracks. She's reclining unnaturally, writing her ex-boyfriend Ian a long iMessage that's equally awkward: "I miss you! I love you! I'm sorry! Please come back," the works. The tequila-laced text message is one run-on sentence that requires three aggressive thumb scrolls to read in its entirety. The blue iMessage fails to send and is demoted to a green SMS text, just like all the others she's sent him since he left her.

Ella gives the girls the finger, which only makes them laugh harder. When she's back in the city, she'll buy a few bottles of wine and some blow to ingest at home, alone. She'll wake up tomorrow with a painful hangover, full of regret over seducing a grieving father and embarrassed by these desperate drunken pleas to Ian, to which he'll never reply.

CHAPTER FIVE

A Half-and-Half God

EYES OF ELLA'S EX-BOYFRIEND Dylan's size are more common to certain species of insects, allowing them a 360-degree view of their surroundings to detect the slightest movements of potential prey. Their exaggerated eyes are critical to their sustenance and survival. One can argue the same for humans with oversized peepers, whose vocation in life is to act.

Dylan's eyes are the catalyst for his landing the lead role in a binge-worthy cable television series in its fifth season on HBO. Of course, network gigs pay bigger money because they're funded by brand name advertising, but he hasn't landed one of those yet. And anyway, in his opinion, the scripts are usually watered down by censored writing and templated plots to attract the general population of sheep who survive on the familiar cop shows, medical dramas, murder mysteries and perfect-family tragedies, aka assorted stories of redemption.

The actor's eyes, however, don't have the same ocular accessibility to his vicinity as certain species of insects. Rather, his eyes entertain his audience with a 360-degree view of his soul: the audience witnesses everything the characters he plays are going through. His soul assumes the mind of the person he's playing, like a sociopath who lives the life of a doting husband and dedicated father, or like prostitutes who gyrate with feigned eagerness in the windowed storefronts of Amsterdam's Red-Light District: they're anybody the world needs them to be.

An avid reader of all books by Eckhart Tolle, Dylan attributes his success and talent to his spirituality. Tolle writes of "pain-bodies," or demons, as they're called in some circles, useless feelings of desire, guilt, worry and anger. Demons focus on the past and future, forever avoiding the one real thing in life: the present moment. Having disassociated his soul from the ceaseless thoughts and base needs of his human mind and body, Dylan has become a master of his emotions and the choices he makes both on camera and in his everyday life. He only calls on his demons consciously, indulging them in a completely aware state of being. Rather than operating on autopilot, as most people do for the entirety of their lives on Earth, he handpicks every move he makes. Perhaps this explains why some people consider actors lost souls searching fruitlessly for an identity, struggling with genuine human connection, when, in Dylan's opinion, those like himself have transcended pre-programmed human behavior. Actors are supermen, at least the ones who've succeeded in their careers. No, they're real-life superheroes. Gods on earth.

In *The Brave One,* inspired by the old 2007 film of the same name with Jodie Foster, he plays a widower turned vigilante avenging the brutal rape and murder of his wife, a political activist who had a seemingly infinite number of enemies. The script is generous with the drama. Dylan has had the opportunity to portray every possible human emotion in the show. Some critics have accused him of overacting, but he's also won two Emmys.

With the success and longevity of the show—he has two more seasons to fulfill before his seven-year contract is up for renewal—comes the risk of being typecast in similar roles for the rest of his career. That, or his audience will struggle to disassociate him from his longstanding character, so that no matter whom he plays in the future, they'll always see him as Eric Bain from *The Brave One.* One way or another, they'll tire of him eventually, the same way he grows bored with all his lovers, breaking their hearts after devastatingly intense affairs he initiates almost as quickly as he terminates.

The risk of becoming irrelevant is one of the main reasons why he keeps his accountant on retainer to manage his money. The accountant, an overweight bald man who's always in a brown Men's Wearhouse suit—he told Dylan once he owns three of the same—dispenses a weekly allowance to Dylan and advises him on various potential investment opportunities, usually in real estate and recently in a startup for cellular agriculture.

Dylan has other exceptional physical features that don't directly land him roles but do help him get laid. For one, he has a fat, uncut cock. Some Americans are repulsed by fore-skin, but rarely are they with his, especially the women he penetrates. And all the men he fucks love blowing him when he's un-showered. There's also his obsessively tailored phy-sique. He's in the gym at least once daily for two hours, fueled by the Whole30 diet fad he follows 365 days a year.

Like *the* Markus and many other public figures, Dylan isn't satisfied with simply maintaining optimal health and fit-ness. He also needs to flaunt the results on Instagram, flexing in sweat-soaked gym shorts that accentuate the outline of his package. The face is handsome but relatively average save the eyes. A button nose by a plastic surgeon in response to an unfruitful start in acting, square jawline slightly crooked from a high school football injury, lips on the thin side. But the eyes. The eyes are his everything.

Dylan is expecting *the* call, the one that almost all B-celeb-rities in television desire more than anything, the one that will elevate their career to the big screen, their fame reaching a height that requires full-time security detail, a call to confirm he's been cast in the highly anticipated film adaption of *The New York Times* bestseller *Twenty Times a Day,* a mommy-porn novel about a middle-aged mother of twin boys with Asperger's who develops a compulsive sexual relationship with her sons' in-home caregiver while her hubby works late hours to avoid his challenged family. Dylan tastes the forthcoming super stardom as strongly as the sugarless Mentos gum he's been popping in his mouth and spitting out every few minutes after the taste of each has lost its flavor—he only allows himself such an unhealthy dessert during times of extreme anxiety.

On this cool spring night in Los Angeles, he wears a black jumpsuit by Henrik Vibskov with no underwear, a pair of mismatched socks, one black from Uniqlo, the other camel-colored with Gucci's brown logo webbing, and sneakers from the latest collection of the Nike/Dark-White collaboration, designed by newly legendary fashion designer, Barbeau. Dylan's wavy, chin-length caramel hair is still damp from a shower as he walks to his car from the two-bedroom guest house he rents in West Hollywood. He has a new MINI Countryman that the auto manufacturer gave him as payment for posting on Instagram two photos and one video of himself driving it.

Leasing two residences, one in Los Angeles, the other in New York, comes with a number of benefits. It gives Dylan the opportunity to audition in person for blockbuster films in L.A. such as *Twenty Times a Day* and lead roles on Broadway, like Stanley Kowalski in a revival of *A Streetcar Named Desire*—which he didn't get—versus sending in audition tapes recorded on his phone. This is all between filming *The Brave One,* of course. He also balances several trysts on both coasts, relinquishing himself of any responsibilities of romance with the excuse that his stay in either city is always temporary, acting is his priority, and nothing serious can develop even if he wanted it to. In truth, he never wants it to.

He made his decision to become bicoastal several years ago, after a tumultuous affair in New York with an unstable woman a bit older than him. Her manic delusions of their relationship took a toll on him and, subsequently, his performances in auditions. It wasn't until he was almost rid of her that he was cast in *The Brave One*, and he's received a steady amount of offers since then. He thinks of her sometimes, mostly with resentment and pity, hoping that she's gotten the help she so desperately needed.

After a few lines of blow and several glasses of Macallan, neat, he's driving to meet a stranger at the Proper Hotel in Santa Monica. He met the dude on Grindr. They only shared body pics, no face, because of a mutual need for discretion, each for different reasons, the details of which neither of them revealed. If, upon meeting, one or the other isn't interested, they'll be on their separate ways without further discussion.

The cocaethylene coursing through Dylan's veins and the forthcoming stranger sex is a much-needed escape from the overwhelming anticipation of *the* call about landing the role for *Twenty Times a Day*. He also just loves getting high and banging hotties. There's always someone to be temporarily in mad love with. This has gotten him into trouble many times, when the intoxicating effect of first kisses have waned and whatever lover of the month is planning their future together. He's left behind countless bodies both on and off camera.

Driving intoxicated is easy for him. Without music playing, he hyper-focuses on the road and the Google Maps lady directing him in her impersonal robotic voice, which he finds oddly comforting—although his semi-erection is a little distracting. The phone rings, jolting him out of concentration. Thankfully, he's already nearing his destination. He exits I-10 onto Lincoln Boulevard, answering a call from his agent while stopped at a red light.

"What up, what up!" the agent shouts like a motivational speaker greeting his gullible acolytes.

"Hey bro, how you been?" Dylan asks, sniffling.

"Good, good, you know, chillin'. Finally done for the day."

"Nice, I'm so fucking glad we're done shooting."

"I'm so happy for you, brother. Getting your dick wet in the meantime at least?"

"Of course. On my way out now, actually." Dylan chuckles, accidentally blowing away the hefty bump of coke on his car key.

"Ha, my man."

"Hell, yeah. But getting a little bored. Dying to hear about this movie... what's the word?"

"Not to worry, my brother. It's going to happen. You *deserve* this role. All the work you've put into *The Brave One*, this is the next step. I feel it in my motherfucking dick, man!"

"No doubt," Dylan replies, his blood pressure rising, as it always does at the prospect of getting what he wants.

Amazing memories of his younger years surface, like the time he did his eighth-grade teacher. Others, a few in particular, have scarred him for life: his crazy ex-girlfriend falsely accusing him of date rape after he'd dumped her. She subsequently committed suicide. The police quickly learned of her mental health issues and that she'd lied about the whole thing, but Dylan's reputation at school was soured for the rest of senior year. His classmates labeled him a player, an asshole. But when he became a TV star, many of the former classmates who'd ostracized him in school wanted to reconnect. And when he lands this massive movie deal, even more will rear their ugly heads.

"Well, uh, 'bout to meet up with someone. Hit me up with the good news soon."

"Yes, brother. Also, construction on my Malibu digs is done, and I'm throwing a party this weekend. Swing by if you can. I'll have Becca send the deets."

"Baller."

"All right then," the agent says, ending the call.

Dylan does a proper key bump, then puts the car into drive.

Through the windowed front of the Proper Hotel, he sees that the lobby lounge, Palma, is packed despite the late hour of his arrival. Outside, a visibly drunk crowd of well-dressed white men and women with wobbly stances are smoking near the valet parking station, screaming and laughing à la chimpanzees. The last thing he needs is one of them recognizing him.

He drives past the hotel and parks on Wilshire, hides a bag of blow in his Gucci sock and leaves the car. He wears a burnt orange ski hat pulled over bushy eyebrows, his lovely hair tucked neatly underneath. Now he just has to avoid eye contact to make it through the lobby undetected. At best, someone may glance his way and observe that he's trying to conceal his identity with the hat and downcast eyes, and that he may be someone famous. That, or just another wannabe assuming celebrity behavior and dress. Either of the two are fine with him, just as long as he isn't positively identified.

His right calf tenses as he enters the building via the side entrance, power walking the length of the lobby, his insect eyes superglued to the natural wood floor. He misses the chic bar adorned with glasses of custom cocktails and smooth elbows of beautiful people. He hardly glances up at the thin, young Mexican-looking guy manning the front desk and who's dressed in all white. The desk is made of some type of off-white stone with a uniquely sculpted texture.

"Hi!"

"Hey man, here for room 209."

"Sure, and your name?" the attendant asks, dialing the room.

The name of Dylan's character in *The Brave One* is the first that comes to mind. "Eric," he says. He prays the attendant doesn't ask him the name of the stranger he's about to mouth fuck because he has no goddamn clue. The overwhelming thought of embarrassing himself is making him lightheaded. His hearing muffles, vision blurs. He sees the attendant's lips moving as he talks into the phone, but he can't make out the words.

The attendant hangs up and says something in Dylan's direction, snapping him out of his trance.

"What's that?"

"Oh! I just said you may go up. Elevators are to the right, behind you. Jack will key you in."

Dylan turns. Another hotel worker dressed in white, presumably Jack, is smiling and ready at the elevators. Dylan walks briskly into the first open car without a word to the front desk attendant or Jack, who follows him in. Jack has the generic good looks and obvious day job of an aspiring actor. These luxury hotels decorate their halls with the sad, beautiful faces of hungry young artists. Swiping his keycard, Jack presses the button for the second floor and exits before the doors slide shut.

"Have a good night, sir," he says in a suspiciously pleasant tone.

"Yeah, you too," Dylan mumbles, wondering if Jack recognizes him.

The door slides shut, and he's alone again, safe from inquiring eyes.

Dylan is like the minotaur trapped in King Minos's maze as he struggles to navigate the tricky layout of the second floor of the hotel. The range of room numbers listed on the walls, with arrows below them pointing in every direction but the right one, and the long stretches of hallway interconnecting two buildings that make up the oddly designed hotel only add to the difficulty of locating the stranger's room. Breaking a light sweat after what feels like a good five minutes of searching, he spots the door to room 209 at the other end of the third or fourth hallway he's stomped down more than once. The glare of recessed overhead lighting just above the door dramatizes a glint in the peephole, the eye of room 209. It could be the coke getting to him, but the peephole looks like a human eye. Did it just blink? More likely, the stranger is operating it from behind the door, evaluating his meat, which is more than fine with Dylan, provided the stranger is at his level of physicality and sucks good cock. Upon knocking, he hears frantic shuffling, sniffles and curses.

"Just a minute," the stranger replies in a slightly effeminate voice that borders on Dylan's threshold for sounding too gay. But he's horny, so he lets it slide.

Thirty seconds later the door flies open to reveal his suitor: a thirty-something man with dirty blond hair, dark brown eyes that look black in the dim light, and a lean and toned body, at least as far as Dylan can gather with the stranger in a relaxed-fit black T-shirt and Nike running shorts. The sweaty face is above average, handsome, but the opaque eyes are clearly bugged from drugs. They're unnaturally oversized but nothing like the actor's own insect eyes that have fostered his relatively successful career. Dylan passes no judgment because he isn't invested in this stranger's well-being or his good looks outside of what he needs tonight. The stranger's crazy, drugged eyes will be closed and watering when his mouth is full.

"Hey," the stranger says.

"What's up."

"Come on in," he says, gesturing to the bed, his left hand dripping blood.

"Dude, your hand."

"Oh fuck, sorry. I was fixing something and cut myself... Well, come in, come in, let me rinse this off real quick."

"Cool, no big deal, just don't get any on me." Dylan, satisfied enough with the stranger's appearance and too horny to be turned off by his sketchy demeanor and inopportune injury, pulls off his jumpsuit and lies on his back on the bed, perpendicular to the head of it. The stranger is in the bathroom scrubbing his hands, sniffling and breathing through his mouth. Dylan is getting an erection from the dysfunctional scene. He eyes the stranger from head to toe. At the stranger's feet, he sees the marble threshold between the bathroom and living space is in pieces, the surrounding carpet in shreds and bloodstained. "What happened there?"

"Oh this? Nothing... want some blow?"

"Yeah, sure. After you do a line off this dick like you said you would." The overly direct come-on snaps the stranger out of his drug-induced anxiety. Instantly calm, he pulls a healthy bag of blow from his gym shorts and approaches Dylan's legs, falling to his knees. The two lock big eyes, Dylan glancing down impatiently, the stranger looking up with hunger. The relaxed expression on the stranger's face shifts to one of great surprise.

"What is it?" Dylan asks.

"Whoa… I know you… Dylan, right?"

Dylan, instantly the more nervous one, doesn't hear in the stranger's tone the excitement of someone who recognizes a celebrity. The effects of the drugs dissolve with the revelation of who the stranger is, and how he knows him.

Earlier that night, from the room directly above her work husband Brandon's, Ella texted him, "OMG the new episode of *Euphoria* is out," while basking in the serenity of her luxurious private space—he'd hooked her up with a king suite. In the newly remodeled landmark building from the twenties with contemporary interior colors and textures inspired by the nearby coastline, she settled into her king-sized bed and favorite TV show. Despite her tranquil surroundings, she was distracted by an unrelenting loneliness that had been haunting her ever since Ian had left her nearly eight months ago. She still hasn't heard from him. The ghosts of all her tragic past relationships have become closer than the soul of her dead brother Frank. Brandon was her last man standing.

CHAPTER SIX

Mr. Snuffleupagus

BRANDON'S LIPS ARE SWOLLEN from the anonymous blowjob he gave earlier in the night, a free and natural alternative to Juvéderm. The effects of the rosé he drank all day in the lobby lounge, toiling away on an ancient company-issued loaner laptop—Pure Creative's tech support team has yet to give him a permanent replacement for the new MacBook Pro he lost in a blackout drunken stupor last Saturday afternoon—are lingering with the taste of the cigarette he smoked by the window after his hookup left. But unsafe sex, or some comparable indulgence, had to be done despite the guilt he's feeling now.

His violent, age-old anxiety for a fix that usually only overpowers him on real holidays, at peak stress levels or whenever he's truly alone, has surfaced on these recurring work-related trips to Los Angeles. After all, he's still in a hotel and far from home, exhausted from prepping for the meeting with Markus and his crew, the Night Army, and the fight in his mind over an uncertain relationship back in New York. His boyfriend is waiting patiently for an answer to his marriage proposal.

Brandon's craving for more pleasure is wildly charged. The pain isn't as physical as an electrical shock, but it's still torturously uncomfortable. The ravenous electric bee of Want is buzz-buzz-buzzing in the pit of his belly, albeit slightly quieter since he ingested the stranger's come. The time on his iPhone turns to eleven p.m., initiating the alarm he set earlier in the day to remind himself to go to sleep at a reasonable hour tonight. He's meeting his co-workers for breakfast in the lobby lounge at seven in the morning to rehearse one last time before the big presentation a few hours later. Unlike his co-workers, Brandon views *Holy War* as just another project, with all the headaches and thrills that come with it. Yes, it's fun hanging around celebrities, and okay, it'd be cool to win awards and make more money because of it. But if he really wanted to star-fuck, he'd just take one of his former *America's Next Top Model* contestant friends to the club to lure in hot bi guys.

The Pure team had met with Markus's crew several times over the past year and a half developing the *Holy War* TV series, but not Markus himself. The show was originally slated to go live three months ago, a year to the day after the *Holy War* music video had premiered. Bad publicity about Markus touching a girl inappropriately during his concert had delayed production because of Telco's morality concerns, so Pure's CEO, Robin, had to get involved to smooth things over as best she could. Markus and Telco have verbally approved the terms of a revised agreement, but nothing has been signed yet. On top of that, Baby kept delaying a face-to-face meeting between Pure and Markus until he was completely confident about the plan for the series. After Telco paid nearly a million dollars in agency fees to the Pure team to act as mediator for the swirl between the parties and to develop the pilot episode to the Night Army's liking, they're finally going to meet Markus. But for Brandon, the fun of the project died shortly after the concert last fall and all the stress and sleepless nights that have followed.

Brandon taps snooze on his phone when the alarm reminding him to go to sleep comes on. He should just turn it off altogether. He won't be in bed for hours, let alone a few more minutes. Must find honey, the electric bee of Want in his belly demands, or rubber to block the transfer of electricity, he counters, knowing all too well that a healthy alternative to his base habits doesn't exist.

Traveling for business comes with some benefits that offset how much it all drains him. He pays for gourmet dinners with his corporate Amex, freeing up his own funds for a variety of naughty fun. He loves treating co-workers generously like a rich someone he isn't. He does okay, though, making six figures but still living paycheck to paycheck on account of his many expenses: rent, clothes, nights on the town, utilities, and one percent of his pay deposited into a 401K quite pathetic for someone in their mid-thirties. On the annual occasions he acquires extra dollars—namely tax season, cost-of-living increases in pay from Pure, and gifts from relatives on his birthday and holidays—he blows it all over the course of the next two weekends, indulging in eight balls and bottle service at Soho House with fair-weather friends.

Despite these circumstances, he isn't self-sabotaging over some PTSD from a bad childhood. On the contrary, he grew up in a middle-class family in the sleepy suburbs of Ohio where the only form of trauma inflicted on him was extreme boredom and a touch of homophobia. Most would label his hedonistic lifestyle an immature abandoning of adult responsibilities, but it's more of a subconscious attempt to counterbalance selling his soul to the cultish advertising industry, indulging in vain consumerism and taking advantage of a safe long-term relationship with a genuinely good person who'll never hurt him and whom his parents love dearly.

His brief yet costly reprieves from The Void come with consequences: morning-after shame; the infamous two-day hangover; the defeated look on his lover's face from their don't-ask-don't-tell agreement around extracurricular sex; and Brandon's best-friends-forever with Guilt for nothing and everything at the same time. Yet none of these repercussions is stopping him from obeying his gut tonight, which is belly-aching orders for more, more, more! With no alternatives coming to mind, he texts his L.A. dealer. His connect, Quinn, lives in downtown L.A., practically a state away during commuter traffic times, but the hour is late, and Uber estimates just twenty minutes from the hotel to downtown.

If this were a normal Monday night at home, lying on the couch with his boyfriend, overeating bad takeout and watching a new episode of his favorite series *Euphoria* would be enough of a fix. Not tonight. Irritated by a notification from Ella, he switches her incoming messages to do not disturb. In an hour or so he'll miss her group text to him and his co-workers that the pre-production meeting has been moved up to six a.m. to accommodate Markus's schedule.

After-hours in downtown Los Angeles is like midtown Manhattan if it were hit by a zombie apocalypse. There seem to be as many permanently closed shops, boarded up high-rises and vacant-eyed homeless people from Skid Row roaming the streets as there are twenty-four-hour delis, new construction in deafening progress and solipsistic workaholics power walking in midtown Manhattan. The one establishment that Brandon knows is open at this hour is a vape store on Sixth Street where he stops to replenish his Juul cartridges—he only smokes the mint-flavored ones.

He limits his visits downtown to absolute necessities, i.e., when he's on the West Coast and needs blow. His *better* local dealer, Cora, who used to meet him anywhere on the west side, doesn't respond to his texts anymore. Once rumored to be Miley Cyrus's dealer, Cora had an epiphany while hallucinating that prompted her to get out of the coke business. She strictly sells magic mushrooms now, which Brandon ingests only when he's far from a city and enjoying nature, preferably alone or in the company of animals.

The dealer's apartment building is locked and guarded by an inattentive doorman in a worn, wrinkled uniform. As usual when he ventures over here, Brandon is puffing on his Juul near the entrance, waiting patiently for someone to leave so he can gain entry. The doorman always glances up but never stops him or asks whom he's there to see, and tonight's no different. A converted warehouse, the massive building encompasses almost half the block. Inside, the long and narrow hallways with uncomfortably high ceilings are giving him anxiety. It's as though the walls are closing in. In times of coke-induced paranoia, he fears there's no way to escape from a cop or robber, but neither has shown himself to date.

At the far end of the hallway, on the eighth floor, Brandon knocks on the apartment door, disturbing the dealer's dogs, two nasty rat-sized mutts whose yapping irritates the hell out of him. He resists the urge to kick when the dealer opens the door and they painlessly attack his ankles.

"Misty, no! April, go to your crate! Go to your crate, I said!" Quinn is an obese guy with a high-pitched voice and a lazy eye. In drag, she's Ms. Quim. Tonight he's Quinn but in a rush to transform into his alter ego before his performance at the club later. "Good evening, Ms. Brandy. I'm rushing to get ready. How many? Three?"

"Yep. What's your Venmo again?"

"Quinnies... that's i-e-s, not y-apostrophe-s. Don't get it twisted, *hunty*."

"Right, right." Brandon loves that he can pay for the drugs digitally and doesn't have to schlep to a sketchy ATM late at night. It's an L.A. thing. In New York, drugs are cash only.

As he pockets the baggies, his anxiety intensifies. He shouldn't be buying this much. Quinn's coke is strong, and he has work in the morning. Quinn says it's fish scale, slang for quality coke, but Brandon's pretty sure it's just cut with speed for a more intense high. Nevertheless, his regret for buying the drugs will pass by the time he exits the building.

The Uber ride back to the hotel will take an estimated twenty minutes, but it already feels much longer. Darkness surrounds the car, save for intermittent streetlights along the highway and scattered lights in the windows of low-rise buildings that make up this sprawling, suburban metropolis. To stave off his impatient need to snort away the two hundred bucks in powdered form that's burning a hole in his Nike gym shorts, he logs on to Grindr, switching the zip code to Santa Monica, in search of men who are online and close to his hotel.

A drunken group of happy hour victims are outside the main entrance to the hotel when he arrives. They're smoking *actual* cigarettes in—gasp—L.A. Their heads rubberneck in his direction as he exits the car. The two girls are gaping shamelessly at him. Before he can escape inside, the shorter of the blond pair grabs him by the arm.

"Um, hi, so my girl over there thinks you're super hot. Want to say hi?"

The other one lowers her head, her hand acting as a visor to hide her flushed cheeks. "Oh my god, Christine, stop!"

"What's up bro," one of the cookie cutter hot dudes interjects. "Want to have a cig with us?" He's wearing a fitted black suit, sans tie or loosened collar.

If he were offering on his own behalf, the answer would be hell yes, but alas... "I'm good, thanks. Your friend is cute, but I'm not into girls," Brandon discloses.

The failed, messy matchmaker drops back her bleached head, roaring at the clear night sky. "Fuck, of course!"

Brandon shrugs, a superficial apology for preferring dick. He rushes inside before having to suffer through more. Perhaps he'll find the hot dude on Grindr later. "Straight, discreet, looking for now."

Like The Flash, Brandon whizzes through the lobby into the first elevator car. He swipes his keycard and hits the button for the second floor. He taps the close button repeatedly as if he were sending an urgent telegram, praying to no one that the doors slide shut before someone else arrives. Shared elevators exacerbate his claustrophobia, especially when he's in a rush to do drugs and find a dude to do him.

This being his third visit to The Proper, he's familiar with the zigs and zags of the hallways and interconnected buildings, barely having to look up at the arrows and range of room numbers at every corner to find his room. The peepholes on the doors are just peepholes, but he knows after a few lines they'll become evil eyes copping his every move, even when he's on the other side of the one living in the door to his room. The eye will just do a 180.

The first hour or so is a pleasure. The beginning of the high motivates Brandon to shower, moisturize, coif and conceal, and dress in his hookup uniform, a plain black T-shirt and gym shorts. Before opening the Grindr app on his iPhone, he answers a few demanding work emails that would've raised his anxiety if he was sober. He responds to the urgent requests from clients and co-workers in an obliging tone that borders on peppy, quite the antithesis to his trademark sass. They reply with emojis of praying hands and bright yellow hearts, pleasantly surprised by his sudden flexibility.

Phase two of his evening begins with two more lines, beer and vodka from the mini fridge, the initial signs of anxiety and paranoia seeping from his brain into his chest, and a tingling in his crotch. He quits all work applications on his laptop, opens Apple Music to play chill but upbeat tunes, specifically the album *Honey* by Robyn. He sets aside the laptop on the other side of the king-sized bed and commences the search on his phone for more strangers. Just as he opens Grindr, a banner notification appears. His boyfriend is texting, likely to say that he's having trouble sleeping without him in bed. Brandon will struggle to sleep tonight, too, but for very different reasons. He thumbs his boyfriend away, mildly annoyed at the inadvertent cock-block, making a mental note to tell him tomorrow that he was already sleeping when he messaged him. "Long day."

Brandon's profile pic on Grindr is from his shirtless torso collection of a couple years ago, when he was single and a few pounds lighter. The tattoos on his arms are visible, which would be a no-no if he were in New York, but he's not. He's thousands of miles away, where he isn't at risk of being recognized by anyone who may know his boyfriend. He's *pretty sure* they agreed to a don't-ask-don't-tell open relationship when they were drunk and high one night last year. He boldly advertises he's looking to suck straight or masculine bi cock. He selects "discreet" as his "tribe" and filters his search to white tops only.

He isn't racist or anything like that; he just isn't attracted to men of color. His preferences may stem from the subconscious racism that comes with being white in America, he realizes, but he doesn't believe it's his fault. He doesn't understand why he should force himself to fuck people he doesn't want just to be politically correct. No one needs to know about the various white boys he enlists to dick him down on whatever night.

Messages pop up every five minutes or so. Sometimes it's from a user with a blank profile who shoots over a cock pic but no face pic. The cock is nice, but then they finally send the face and it's all over. It's been at least an hour of back and forth to the bathroom to snort lines, then the mini fridge for another beer, the paranoia growing with every beat of his overworked heart. Did the peephole blink? He's tempted to peek through the hole to see if anyone is on the other side peeping his fevered actions, but he isn't there yet. He will be soon.

Others say they aren't looking for tonight. It's Monday night, and they have work tomorrow, as does Brandon, but he's in pseudo-vacation mode and the morning of responsibility is the last thing on his mind. He messages other torsos with a canned message saved on the app that explains his needs for the night, so he doesn't have to retype the same thing hundreds of times. Like anything else—fishing, auditioning, pitching new business—the hookup hunt is a numbers game. But by now he's a sweaty mess from the blow, as if he's having the workout of a lifetime. He'll have another shower and change his outfit before anyone comes over.

Finally someone bites, a hot torso with a great cock. One of the guy's photos reveals the lower half of his face with its fine jawline and good lips. He's the one. They exchange few words, just enough to get their points across. The conversation ends with Brandon sharing his address and the torso replying with an ETA of twenty minutes.

The confirmation of a visitor initiates the second shower of the night, which proves to be difficult. He jumps out every minute or two to check the door, leaving a sopping wet foot trail from the tiled bathroom floor through the carpeted living/sleeping space. Eventually he gives up, leaving the stall for the last time without completely rinsing off the Aesop body wash in his crotch and ass. At least he'll smell extra fresh. Patting himself dry, he checks the time. He has about five minutes left to moisturize, coif, conceal and dress again, so he rushes to get it done in two, leaving himself three minutes to do another line before hiding the evidence. He doesn't know a) if this guy parties, b) if he's a cop or robber, or c) both a and b. Scrambling to find a hiding space, he settles on a small opening in the floor between the marble threshold of the bathroom and the doorframe. He drops the bag of coke in it and gets to tidying up.

He wipes the coke crumbs off the bathroom sink with the palm of his hand and licks them clean. He collects the empty beer cans and tiny vodka bottles, placing them neatly on top of the mini fridge. In front of the wardrobe, he piles high the clothes that were strewn about the room. He dims the lights and flips Robyn over to Frank Ocean, lowering the volume so it's less of a soundtrack for the forthcoming sex and more just background noise to fill the uncomfortable silence of strangers meeting and fucking. One of his pet peeves is when his bobbing head syncs with the bass of the music.

Cocaine comes back to mind. He can use one more line before sex. Dropping to his knees at the bathroom entrance, he sticks his finger in the space between the corner of the doorframe and the marble threshold where he dropped the coke. Digging around inside, he realizes the hole is much deeper than he thought. His finger barely grazes the tip of the plastic baggie of powdered salvation. He's pushed it deeper into the hole, so it's now well under the threshold and out of reach. His heart is speeding to the point of reckless endangerment.

"Fuck fuck fuck!" He must hurry. The guy will be here soon.

Rummaging through a toiletry bag, he finds his tweezers and shoves them in the hole in the hopes of getting a grip on the baggie, but to no avail. When he pulls out his finger, it's bloody from scraping it against a nail in the floor. The tweezers are bent out of shape and permanently unusable. He chucks them across the room and resorts to pulling up the carpet that borders the marble threshold, revealing an unfinished wood platform. From there he's able to grip the threshold with his clammy hands and pull with all his might. The Equinox classes that Ella is always dragging him to have paid off. The marble breaks into two pieces, one of them cutting his palm. The force of the release propels him backward, causing him to hit his head on the edge of the bed frame. Dazed and determined, he thrusts himself back up to his knees. He scans the wreckage for his Precious, and there it is, covered in blood. Luckily, the baggie was shut tightly, so the blow hasn't been contaminated.

After rinsing his hands, which refuse to stop bleeding, he uses a hand towel to block the blood flow and awards himself with a fat rail of coke. He gets back on his knees to piece the bloody marble threshold back together like a gruesome puzzle. He wipes it down and smooths the carpet back in place as best he can. At first glance, the destruction isn't noticeable, so he should be able to get away with it. By the time the hotel staff, or perhaps the next guest, discovers it, it'll be impossible to determine who did it. It could've been anyone who used this room previously or will in the future.

By the time the front desk calls, informing him of his guest's arrival, he's a sweaty mess again. The last soaked T-shirt, chilled by the air conditioning on full blast, is a lovely cooling agent for his overheated brow. He darts into the bathroom for one last beauty check in the mirror, and notices he needs a little more concealer to hide his puffy eyes and darkening circles. The guy knocks on the door as he's blending in the makeup with the tip of a shaky digit.

"Deep breath," he tells his reflection. The well-practiced smile that lifts his features and a few years of age comes into view. The Botox he had injected about a week and a half ago is in full effect, so his crow's feet are nowhere to be found. He's ready for what's behind door number-one.

"Okay, Brandon. Let's do this."

The sweet sound of Frank Ocean singing "Chanel" wakes Brandon from his violently induced slumber. His hand and the back of his head are throbbing. The delayed pain has arrived, causing him to wince audibly. The water is running in the bathroom sink, the air in the room cold against his freezing, vibrating skin. His heart is pounding, and he's wet with sweat and blood. The night comes back to him like the scent of a memory. Pulling himself up by the end of the mattress, he struggles to stand fully because his shorts and boxer briefs are constricting his ankles. He remembers Dylan and starts to cry.

The track flips to "Nights," the lyrics apropos of his cruel, secretive encounter with Dylan. The difference between the story in the song and what's happened in real life is that Frank's reluctant tryst was ultimately consensual. With Dylan, it turned into anything but. Brandon rolls over in tears, the condom protruding from his anus lightly slapping his inner thigh. He flinches at the stinging sensation as he pulls it out, noticing it's ripped.

He casts back to the time he blew the quarterback in high school in someone's basement during a house party. The next day Brandon told everybody, so he wasn't shocked when the football player and his teammates jumped him in retaliation for spreading the "lie." Brandon took the beating in silence. Having hid his effeminacy as best he could when he was a kid, he rarely received a sideways look, let alone a classmate calling him a fag. He'd always wondered what it was like being gay-bashed, but he never thought it'd be instigated by his own actions. It's no wonder he's lying on the floor, soaking up the carpet with his blood and tears, blaming himself for Dylan's attack. He should've known better than to say Dylan's name, acknowledge who he is. Even if Dylan had recognized him before Brandon called him out, he'd have acted like he hadn't. Discreet means discreet, and Brandon didn't hold up his end of the bargain.

He considers calling 911 but decides against it. There are drugs somewhere in the room, unless Dylan took the baggie. Bottles are everywhere. The floor near the bathroom is in shreds. What's more, this is a business trip, and Pure would surely fire him for this. He's not positive Dylan raped him, anyway. He could've been obliging after Dylan chucked him into the door. But then a flashback of the sock in his mouth, his wrists cuffed with Dylan's large hand. Faggot this and faggot that. "If you say something to anyone, I will fucking ruin you." The common line in movies and TV shows that depict rape and sexual assault proved to be accurate. Or perhaps Dylan was playing a role influenced by cinema.

The clock on the nightstand reads after midnight. Brandon rinses his hands, sops up the blood on the back of his head with two white hand towels, staining them crimson. He tosses them in the trash, covering them with a ball of toilet paper. With a desperate urge to get out of the room, he exits without looking in the mirror to see the bloody, torn black T-shirt, the semen stains on his shorts hardening and turning white.

He's just walking. He's walking and humming "Nights" by Frank Ocean and just strolling down the hall without a care in the world. Adrenaline has replaced his craving for more coke. He's higher than ever.

In the elevator, a lesbian couple, both with long braids and matching white and camel-colored linen outfits, stand aghast at his appearance, but he doesn't notice. He's just riding the elevator, minding his own business. They ask him if he's okay, but their concerned voices fall on deaf ears. "Nights" is blaring from the speakers in his brain.

The doors open and he walks out slowly. The couple rushes past him to get help from the front desk. He exits enveloped in Frank's singing voice, consumed by the intensifying natural high. But then he collapses, and as his face meets the hard lobby floor, he feels absolutely nothing.

In a thinly veiled judgmental tone, the police officers take Brandon's statement from his hospital bed. He doesn't immediately reveal that it was Dylan who hurt him. After he tells them that he met the guy on Grindr, they don't bother asking whether he knew his attacker. He wouldn't have gone to the cops anyway if he hadn't passed out in public, but he figures blaming the damage to the room on a rapist versus his own coked-up doing is a better alibi than the truth. "This thing happens all the time," they tell him in soft, condescending voices. He keeps his mouth shut when the nurse administers the various tests of a rape kit, hoping they don't find any of Dylan's come. He just wants this to be over. That said, if the security cameras at the hotel have anything to show for it, Dylan will be recognized, and it'll all be over for him and his B-list fame.

If Brandon's doctor hadn't refused to discharge him until she was sure his concussion was gone, he'd be on the next plane home to New York right about now. Instead, he's stuck on this uncomfortable hospital bed, sharing a room with an old man who has an offensive smell and a deafening snore, while the boyfriend sends dozens of worried texts throughout the day.

"Why didn't you say good morning back? Are you working?"

"Okay, now you're scaring me, where the fuck are you?"

"Um, Ella is freaking out. She said you didn't show up to meetings today. You better not be hungover in your hotel room. We talked about this."

"Seriously, where are you?"

The boyfriend's melodramatic messages and Link and Ella's stern voicemails keep on coming. Brandon ignores them all. He'll respond after he's invented an excuse for his disappearing act. The truth about Dylan will be too much for them to handle, especially Ella. She's still not over him and probably never will be, as evidenced by the myriad drunken rants she's been giving for the nearly two years Brandon has known her.

A blanket of exhaustion covers Brandon's ankles, then his legs, torso, neck and head. He needs a day off, to join in on the stinky old man's horrible snoring. In a way he's relieved he's here, for once taking a real break from work and play—and with a valid doctor's note to boot. His time as executive producer on *Holy War* may be over, but there'll be other big projects soon, he's sure. He should just accept the boyfriend's proposal, settle down and have children. He should grow up. Thoughts of quitting advertising and moving to a cushy job on the brand side of things wash over him like the effects of the one Alcoholics Anonymous meeting he and Ella joined after one particularly intense weekend binge. As he drifts off, he makes a promise to himself to—

CHAPTER SEVEN

His Girls

MARKUS ASSUMED that the girl's curves and Kylie Cosmetics smile meant yes. He ran the palms of his soft hands along either side of her. The more he manhandled her, the more hysterical the crowd's eardrum-popping cheers became. A rainbow-patterned tube top two sizes too small accentuated her seventeen-year-old A-cups. By the time he got around to asking the girl what her name was, it was impossible to hear her reply. She spoke something with a "ka" sound into his mic. Was it Rebecca? Jessica? He wasn't sure.

Not even now, when a video of him fondling and kissing the girl during his performance in Colorado, while on his North American tour several months ago, has suddenly gone viral. Disclosing the name of someone underage goes against the policy of most publications, and she never came forward on her own.

As with all other bad press and misinformed accusations, he's chosen to remain mum on Colorado. He refuses to acquiesce to the press, his fans or, privately, to the marketing team at Telco. They told his DJ and business manager, Baby, that they have concerns about continuing their partnership with him on the *Holy War* TV docuseries and would like him to give a statement to the press to smooth things over. They even went so far as to request that a morality clause be added to the contractual terms they've been negotiating for the better half of a year now, to which Markus responded with, "Fuck you"—and which Baby filtered as a polite no.

In Markus's opinion, morality is subjective. Fuck Telco. Colorado aside, the uptight company could claim a breach of contract for half the shit he does, such as his derogatory lyrics about girls and gays. Telco's un-woke marketing team doesn't know crap about rap. He isn't prejudiced in real life. Everyone knows how much he loves the ladies, and he lets dudes blow him—including that blond androgynous supermodel—when he's in a certain mood. Plus, he's known publicly as being half Black. In truth, the few Black relatives he has are unrelated by blood, but he keeps this to himself. Regardless, if Telco isn't going to stand by him when some bullshit story like the Colorado girl comes out, how will they handle something real? Their antiquated reaction to it has left a bad taste in his mouth, but Baby says he needs the good press that'll come with the *Holy War* series to circumvent the rising rumors of sexual misconduct, so he should try to sort things out with Telco. "Even though the girls are all lying, gold-digging chicken heads," he adds smartly.

Public outcries and Baby's white lies aside, what Markus did onstage isn't illegal in the state of Colorado where the incident occurred, so no one is pressing charges. One way or another, the assault on his celebrity status will die down, just like the previous incidents. The Colorado girl will never work out the rest of their night together. He usually reserves such bad fun for home, but he desperately needed to get off that night. At the "after party" he recorded with a well-hidden iPhone in the penthouse suite of the Ritz-Carlton Denver, his wingmen were GHB and MDMA.

Markus stores his many secret recordings in an impenetrable safe in the panic room of his Bel-Air mansion. It's the sole place in his home without retractable glass walls or windows and is only accessible via a hidden door in one of his ten and a half bathrooms. All the bathrooms have identical stark white minimalist décor. The one exception is the master bathroom, which boasts a color scheme of matte black and gold leaf, and an oversized portrait of Markus shot by Richard K. In the photo, he's naked and squatting over a bidet with a dirty grin on his dewy face. His legs are crossed, so that they're covering his junk—coincidentally, K, a photographer, filmmaker and writer who came up in New York in the '80s, has had his own share of legal issues with the ladies.

Whenever Markus is home, he'll replay the videos to unwind from a night of debauchery. He'll masturbate alone or get blown by one of his lingering friends who are too high and busy working on him to notice who's in the video on his laptop. She could be Rebecca/Jessica or one of the dozen or so other girls with whom he's had the on-camera pleasure. Most of them are barely legal, but he tastes the vintage ones a few times a year too. In the videos, they're lying naked and unconscious, dreaming of marrying him, *the* Markus, one of their biggest idols since middle school. One of them was still *in* middle school when he filmed her, but that was a special occasion: his twenty-first birthday.

Markus shakes off the thoughts of his girls to concentrate on his morning routine: three sets of curls with thirty-pound dumbbells, twelve reps each, ten minutes on the row machine and as many crunches and pushups he can stand. He thinks this is all he needs to do to maintain a picturesque physique, one that merits ogling his average body in the floor-to-ceiling mirrors in his bedroom every morning. But beneath his ego-centric surface lies the truth. He's a five-foot-seven man with an average-sized penis and a small gut that moonlights as a sixpack when he sucks it in long enough for a camera lens to flutter.

Whether he parties or goes to bed early, he's religiously up and at 'em at the exact time of sunrise noted in the weather app on his phone. His personal assistant, White Lexi—who also happens to be his cousin—knows to plan his day around the sun. He takes his selfies, then sends them to her to do her magic. She gets up at five a.m. every day, ready and waiting to nip, tuck and accentuate his photos in all the right places as quickly as she can before posting them to his Instagram.

This morning, as usual, he captures a few good-morning selfies for his four million Instagram followers, flexing in Calvin Klein boxer briefs. He just inked a deal with the fashion label and is featured on their legendary billboard between Broadway and Lafayette in Manhattan. In the ad, the faux bulge in his boxers leaves little to the imagination. After the self-love, he showers and gets ready for a day of meetings.

White Lexi texts "Happy birthday, cuz" and reminds him that he has a ten a.m. business breakfast at Onda in the Proper Hotel in Santa Monica. He'll be meeting the agency working on *Holy War* to review the run-of-show for the pilot episode. And, of course, his annual birthday blowout will kick off at seven tonight. In the distance, he hears the event production company vans pulling up. He replies to her with a thumbs-up bitmoji that he designed in his likeness, followed by, "Get your fat ass out my pool house, someone's pulling up." She retorts with an eye-roll smiley face and a thumbs-up.

Since puberty, he's found unconscious women unbelievably sexy. White Lexi's family lived on the same street as his in the affluent town of Westchester—Baby and the rest of his team, the Night Army, were raised nearby, too. Markus had sex with White Lexi when they were teens, after she'd passed out from a healthy mix of Percocet and vodka that he'd served her at a keg party in the woods behind their houses. The next day she woke up on the forest floor with a hammering headache, covered in dead leaves. She was still out of it, couldn't remember what had happened. The lower half of her body was raw and sore. It was as if she'd just woken up from an invasive surgery, still groggy from the anesthesia. She ran to Markus's house in tears and told him that something bad had happened to her, but she didn't know what exactly. He convinced her she'd probably just been too drunk to remember hooking up.

Markus grew up anything but poor, despite his Wikipedia biography detailing otherwise. His father was a successful composer and lyricist for A-list musicians in the '70s and '80s. His mother is a recently retired psychoanalyst who used to keep their rich neighbors as patients. They were mainly housewives who suffered from moderate depression in the suburbs of New York, while their husbands commuted to the city every day and got head after work from the occasional call girl in hookup hotels or from lower-level employees in the husbands' pied-à-terre apartments. His parents were upper middle-class with a million or two in the bank and solid connections in the entertainment business, but the struggling artist sob story has sold more albums. His oblivious fans seem to ignore the facts of his background, which can easily be learned via a simple Google search.

Markus got his start when Nickelodeon cast Baby and him in a preteen sitcom about navigating the trite tribulations of middle school. Markus's father had a connection at the network and arranged the auditions. During filming for the second season of the show, Markus posted a mixtape of his pop-rap on YouTube, and it went viral. He quit acting, signed with Young Blood Records and released his first album, which debuted at number one on the US Billboard 200. The rest is history—a phrase about as cliché as his path to superstardom, he realizes, but at the same time, he doesn't give a crap because it's true. He graciously brought Baby and the rest of his childhood friends along for the ride, albeit as his employees. Their relationships went off-kilter after that, but, eventually, everyone acclimated to their new lives in Markus's world.

With the fame has come a new kind of adversity: the public overanalyzing his every move, judging him without the facts. He's been feeling more vulnerable with the recent accusations of his treatment of women. The more he's celebrated, the worse the allegations get. He doesn't claim to be innocent, but the stories have all been bullshit gossip from anonymous sources—so far anyway—and the one columnist who hinted at having more on him than rumors took a bribe.

For the most part, he's been careful, and the Night Army will always be there to alibi his ass or step in as a witness in his defense. Also, his PR team keeps informants on retainer at all the major gossip rags. They give his team a shout whenever an unfavorable article about him is in the works, giving Baby time to halt publication with a discreet cash offer or juicier news about someone else—which is why Markus has White Lexi discreetly record his famous friends misbehaving at his scandalous parties.

The girl from the ad agency is a skinny devil in a pale blue prairie skirt with a pattern of tiny black orchids printed on it. She's also wearing a sleeveless mock-neck tank cut short at the bottom to show off her tiny white girl waist. The face is cute. Other than the dark hair, she's just Markus's type. Her ear-to-ear smile and assertive hello isn't fooling him. He smells the insecurity and anxiety oozing out of every pore, every orifice. He would love to lick her down. Submissive fucked-up girls hiding behind a confident face are his weakness. He sees right through her, and not just because she's so thin and white that she's almost transparent.

"Sup," he replies with a nod, returning her attempt at a firm handshake. He holds on a second longer than is customary, his subliminal way of saying he'd choke her out in bed, just the way she likes it.

"Please, have a seat. We're just so happy to finally meet you," she says.

They're at Onda, a new interculinary restaurant in the Proper Hotel that's having an "It moment" as a hotspot for the rich and famous. The space is shockingly sterile: all white dining room, brilliant concrete floors and a wide-open kitchen that flaunts a grotesque vertical roasting spit of turkey flesh. He bets the girl thought she was smart holding the *Holy War* meeting here, probably having read somewhere about his love of white minimalistic décor and furnishings.

The general manager closed the restaurant to the public for the afternoon on account of Markus's arrival.

Sometimes he reflects on his magnificent position in society, chuckling at his version of a normal life. There's no doubt in his mind that he deserves it. His music touches millions around the world. His work has changed lives, given his fans hope, love and comfort with each chart-topping album or "lost" collection of demos he cranks out every six to eight months. They chant his lyrics from stadiums and lip-sync his songs on their morning commutes via car or public transport. He motivates athletes at the gym and serenades lovemaking and rough fucking alike. They blast his shit at Oscar parties in the Hollywood Hills and from the screen-cracked iPhones of city housing dwellers stuck in Bushwick, making plans for their own holy war. All because of his music. He's a motherfucking *movement*, the catalyst for living selflessly and woke. The charitable good balances out any bad juju he may harbor from his naughty fun with a handful of girls. He's helped the females exponentially more than he's hurt them, so no one can say a word. He'll never stop, let alone ever confess.

Ella is the name of the girl from the ad agency, which he'll remember for however long it takes to get her on her back. She moves her thirsty lips, introducing the rest of her team, going on about the show, the star-studded yet unexpected lineup of his celebrated "friends" and the list of expectations on his part. "So, we're absolutely thrilled to present you with some fun thought-starters for your Instagram posts promoting the show."

He says nothing, which is all his face reveals too. Yes, he knows she's a dumb ass for thinking he'd ever allow some ad agency to direct his Instagram—the only one who can post on his behalf is White Lexi—but he'll let his team respond to that shit. Besides, he's too busy daydreaming of having his way with her while she's completely knocked out on the little bed in his study, the eyes of the hidden high-quality cameras documenting seemingly every inch of her. Still, aligning on a solid activation plan for the *Holy War* mission is critical, but that's why he's paying White Lexi to sit over there, frantically taking notes like a crackhead, while his man Baby pushes back on all of Pure's bullshit.

"Like we agreed when we signed the term sheet," Baby replies, "Markus will promote the show organically. In other words, however and whenever he sees fit. Maybe this isn't going to work. This deal can disappear with one call to our lawyers. Telco's reaction to the Colorado incident has already made us question this venture."

Ella's eyes fill with anxiety. Her poker face falls, revealing the scared little girl waiting in the wings, just as Markus predicted. Her face is saying to him, "God, if I mess up this deal it's my sweet ass." It's saying to the semi-hard cock in his baggy Prada shorts, "I'll do anything."

"I deeply apologize for any miscommunication. Markus has *complete* control. These are extremely loose guidelines—

not even guidelines really, just *suggestions* on how he might choose to promote the—"

"Where's your producer, by the way?" Baby interjects. "We were expecting to see the production schedule today."

"I ha-have it right here. He had a family emergency, um, a sudden death in the family, so he couldn't make it. But the plans are solid, as is our creative and production team. I'd be happy to walk you through—"

"Baby, let's head," Markus says, speaking for the first time since saying hello.

The table goes silent.

"But—Ally is it?"

"Close enough," she says, giggling nervously.

"It's my birthday party tonight, so I'm in a good mood and want to give you a second chance to convince me y'all got your shit together."

Markus stands, his erection concealed behind an oversized black Balmain windbreaker. The girl barely hides her excitement over the personal invite as he looks around the table at the rest of her team, white boys with basic style and fuck-all for names—aka Link and his underlings.

"Yes, yes of course. We'll get the details from Baby."

"No 'we.' Just you," he corrects, tossing on his sunglasses and walking away without another word like the baller he is. He'll see to her later.

"Happy birthday, bro!" yells the Jewish-looking junior creative on Link's team who's rocking last year's Nike Daybreak Undercover gear.

Onda's general manager scurries over to usher a silent Markus and team up the elevator and through the lobby doors. Outside, Markus's bodyguard, Jay, mistakes the manager for the paparazzi, shoving him back with the rest of them. Markus and team slide into their cars. As they speed off, he hears the general manager yelling pleas of gratitude from somewhere within the crowd of greedy photographers and their flashing lights.

At the birthday party in Markus's mansion, White Lexi taps his shoulder. She knows how much it annoys him, but it's impossible to get his attention. She's been screaming his name from right behind him but to no avail. The aggressive volume of the music and surrounding crowd of fake friends of stage and screen are overpowering. The actor Anton-something and some country-pop-singing Amazonian blond ditz are blocking her from getting in front of his face. She has no choice but to jump up to reach over their shoulders and tap him. Seemingly in slow motion, she lands back on her feet. Her body goes stationary except for that fat sexy ass still jiggling. He turns, pushing Anton aside with a mischievous grin and a pat on the shoulder. The singer sneaks a goodbye kiss on Markus's cheek.

"Great to see you, Swiffy," he says, patting her skinny ass. When they've turned away, he looks down at White Lexi. "What did I tell you about coming up on me from behind. You know I hate that shit."

"Sorry, I know, but I've been trying to get over to you for a while. That girl Ella's been waiting in your room."

He responds with a puzzled look.

"The *girl*."

His interest is piqued, but his recollection of who Ella is evades him.

White Lexi pauses, exhaling her frustrations as discreetly as possible. "From the ad agency... the *Holy War* meeting earlier?"

"Oh, fuck yeah. My bedroom or the study?"

She smirks, letting out a baby snort. "You think I don't know you by now?"

"Good girl," he says with a gracious fist bump and slap on the ass.

He spends another twenty minutes snailing his way through the mob of guests. They're either trying to wish him a happy birthday with a selfie to post for bragging rights, gush over how fit he's looking with their please-ass-fuck-me eyes, or brown-nose him with gifts like this custom clock from Dark-White's home collection that this cock-gobbling fashion designer Barbie or Barbeau is handing to him.

"For you, hot stuff!" he announces, his giant hands clasped politely at his waist like a beauty school graduate. "I designed it just for you. See how it matches perfectly to the shade of white on your wall? We know how much you love your white minimalism, so we made sure we had the exact color, thanks to your lovely assistant."

Markus kisses him on the cheek while noticing White Lexi has been following him, so he takes the opportunity to order her to hang it immediately. He doesn't love the font or the shade of white and will probably make her take it down when he wakes up with an angry hangover, but it's fine for now. He just wants the girl in his study, whoever she is.

Markus opens the door to the panic room, aka his study, where a skinny girl who looks like she's in her late twenties but is probably older is pacing the room. The girl—whom White Lexi reminded him is named Ella before he walked in— is in a white midi-dress with spaghetti straps and open back designed by Dark-White, the fashion house that the giant fag Barbeau helms. The thing fits like a glove on her slinky figure. His lustful eyes fall to her feet. She's barefoot, and he doesn't immediately see where she left her shoes. A restless big toe is thumb wrestling the toe next to it.

"Hey! Nice to see you again," she chirps, fingering her shiny hair.

"Sup, Ella. Grab a seat." He gestures toward the little bed.

"Interesting room for a study… seems more like a secret dungeon," she replies, still standing. Her eyes enlarge as she cups trembling hands over juicy lips. "Oh my god, oh my god,

I'm *so* sorry. That is *so* unprofessional, I just... I'll admit, I'm a little nervous."

"All good," he consoles, glancing around the space. "It was built to be a panic room, not that I've ever used it for that." Bowing his head in a chuckle, he nestles his chin in the crook of his right hand. "But it's soundproof, and I need the quiet."

"Oh my God, yeah. Like, I can't imagine how hard it is for you to be truly alone."

He nods.

The girl sighs with relief as she sits on the edge of the twin-sized bed, while he fixes their drinks on a mirrored bar cart with gold-plated wheels.

"Some nose candy up in that nightstand," he reveals, much to her excitement. Without fail, all the white girls love the blow.

The nightstand is fantasy-purple with a cartoon portrait of Princess Aurora from Walt Disney's *Sleeping Beauty* painted on its side. It looks misplaced in the otherwise stark white room with mirror and gold accents. Some may think the nightstand is better suited beside the bed of a sleepy little girl, but, in Markus's opinion, his dungeon serves a similar purpose. The nightstand is right where it should be.

Markus loves sleeping girls and all their vulnerabilities. As they lie there in his little bed, knocked out cold from his wing-men, their beautiful faces drooped and drooling, bodies frozen in anticipation of his entry, he's overwhelmed with the feeling of power, of being able to put it anywhere. Sure, most fangirls will do the same awake, but with the little whores wriggling around beneath him, it's less stimulating. He wasn't kidding a moment ago when he said he needed silence, and that especially goes for sex.

When he finally chooses a girl to bear his children, he'll bang her raw while she's conscious, so when she gets a positive pregnancy test, she'll know it's his. After she's given birth, he'll get her more hooked on coke than she was when they met. He'll hire a private detective to document her ho-life, then he'll get a lawyer from the best, win his kid from the judge and send her ass to rehab. He'll get full custody because of her whoring around and of who he is, an A-list star on top of the world. When she's gone, he'll hire some old hag to nanny his son—that's right, son, his load only makes alphas—who'll clean up the boy's literal shit while Markus primes him for a life of power and privilege.

As a flushed Ella grabs greedily at the kilo of nose candy in the nightstand, Markus introduces his wingmen to her drink. He spins around with a bad boy grin and makes his next move.

CHAPTER EIGHT

His Soft Death

FRANK SAVED ELLA'S LIFE many times, both physically
and mentally. He was her only family after their parents died,
acting as her mentor, role model and father figure. Then he
died, too. As each year passes, her recollection of his face gets
blurrier. In the few photos she has of him—their atypical parents failed to document their upbringing—he looks like a
stranger. The story of her brother's death has been reduced to
gossip that she blabs about after one too many. And every
time she does talk about it, her memories of him get more
diluted. It's almost as if he never existed. They've become par-
ables from the bible of a bad religion, like the early Tori Amos
albums that acted as Ella's bible as a teenager. The same can
be said for the stories about her lost lovers, especially Dylan,
but unlike the handful of broken hearts from which she suffered greatly and recovered over the years, her grief over
Frank's death has yet to show mercy. On the flip side, she

rarely thinks of her parents. It was always Frank and her, even when their parents were alive.

Frank saved her from some older kids who attacked her one day after summer school in eighth grade—it was either that or be held back another year. She was cutting through the neglected parking lot of an abandoned Down's Syndrome care center. Had she taken the longer route of Nichols Avenue where there were lots of cars and people around, she'd have been safer, despite the street being notoriously dangerous because it didn't have a sidewalk. One of her classmates had recently been killed there by a hit-and-run. She hadn't been friends with him but knew who he was because he'd been cute and popular. There were racist rumors going around that his death had been gang related because his friends were Black and Puerto Rican.

The eroded parking lot of the clinic was a cracked and crumbling mess. Jagged pieces of sun-faded black asphalt jutted upward as if the lot had been hit by an earthquake, but that would've been unlikely in Connecticut. The long and lean weeds growing through the cracks in the pavement were the real cause of the damage. Their ragged leaves were dull green, as if the golden rays of the summer sun had faded them. As she walked through the eerily silent property, she observed a concrete playground to the left of the building's entrance. The center of the lot boasted a rusty metal swing set, monkey bars and a slide, on which innocent children would never play again.

The exit on the other end of the vast parking lot came into view as she turned the corner by the playground. On her left, a thundercloud of crows abruptly vacated a weeping willow tree. In tandem and equally aggressive as the black birds taking flight, three teenaged boys hopped the fence at the perimeter of the property. They were drinking forty-ounce beers and laughing obnoxiously. At that age, Ella preferred St. Ides malt liquor over Olde English, but both would make her puke now.

The boys' fashion styles varied greatly. The short fat one with a chipped front tooth wore a graphic T-shirt with "Chronic Overdose" on the front of it in a graffiti-style font. Below the words was a closeup of a super-high guy sticking out his tongue. The tall boy with dark brown dreads and JNCO jeans with fabric inserts gave her more of a raver vibe. The muscle dude had an oxymoronic grunge/jock thing going on.

They almost raped her. They succeeded in sexually assaulting her, for sure, and one could argue that the fat one raped her. That is, if just-the-tip is considered rape. Her big brother Frank and his best friend Clay, who were taking the shortcut home after a long day of work at the body shop, cut short the drunken sexual examination of all things Ella. They'd thrown back a few beers themselves and were in a rowdy mood, ready for a fuck or a fight, and ended up indulging in the latter. They beat those rapist pigs so badly that they all remained in the hospital for two-plus months. One of them nearly died, twice. Eighteen-year-old Clay was doubly violent as Frank, his anger fueled by his possessiveness over twelve-year-old Ella—unbeknownst to her brother, she and Clay had been having sex in secret.

When her attackers were questioned by the police, they pretended like they hadn't seen their muggers, claimed they'd been jumped from behind. Frank and Clay hadn't called the police themselves because Clay had a record from drug possession, although it had only been an eighth of an ounce of weed. The judge had sentenced him to community service but had warned that if he broke the law again, she'd toss him in jail for at least a year. After a wave of press around the mysterious assault of three innocent neighborhood boys in the old, abandoned Down's Syndrome care center, urban legends of the place grew and multiplied: ghosts of abused patients haunting the property, cannibalistic melon heads—small humans with bulbous heads, a penchant for violence and an appetite for their own kind—on the prowl, or Black gang members loitering about, as frequently suggested by white people.

Frank and Ella never talked about that day. Had they told their parents, their father would've found a way to blame the rape on their mother, perhaps by saying she taught her daughter to be a whore, turning her mildly violent toward him, with him following suit that much more terrifyingly. Any parental comfort Ella had been seeking wouldn't have been fulfilled, so there was no point in telling them. She and Frank resigned to recovering from the incident by trying to pretend it'd never happened.

And Frank saved her in a very different way from their parents' deaths by murder/suicide, a drunken fight that had ended with their father beating their mother to death and then hanging himself in the basement. That old thing. That old... *thing* that'll live on in her subconscious for the rest of her life, whispering evil advice, influencing her choices—major and minor—and feeding on the nutrients for her mind and body. Perhaps this explains the horrible diet of sour candy and Diet Coke that she followed then and still does when she's stressed out.

Frank was nearly twenty-two then, Ella fifteen. He'd discovered spirituality via LSD and the books of Ram Dass that his pseudo-hippie friends had recommended. According to Dass, psychedelics were the first of three stages to reach spiritual awakening. When Frank dropped acid, he jump-started the larger part of his brain, which, prior to LSD, had lain dormant since his birth. The drug gave him clarity, the ability to see the bigger picture around his parents' violent deaths at his father's hand. He was able to realize that their deaths were a gift to him and his sister. Their cruel parents had been horrible alcoholics, just as addicted to each other as they'd been to their cases of beer and wine. Frank and Ella had always played second fiddle to their tumultuous affair and endless drinking.

Frank developed a better understanding of his purpose in the universe, to which he suddenly felt so connected. His studies broadened: philosophy, psychology, sociology. Despite his dropping out of high school, he became wiser and more self-aware than most college graduates. He had his sister to care for and didn't take that responsibility lightly. They were one another's only family, but her personal Great Depression and anorexia was threatening to kill that off too.

She'd stopped having sex with Clay, ignoring his multiple attempts to continue their secret tryst, and started cutting herself, doing her best to conceal the wounds with long-sleeved shirts and pants, even in the dead of summer. Never a skirt, never a dress, let alone a bathing suit. No one would've found out if she wasn't bleeding through her white sleeves while Frank drove her to school that morning. She quickly realized it hadn't been the best wardrobe choice, but she hadn't been sleeping well on account of the nightmares, so her cognition was less than fresh. The motive for the cutting wasn't as simple as saying she was just trying to feel something. She wasn't that self-aware yet. The cutting was... animalistic. Like a crazed monkey, she'd been reduced to self-biting, feeling caged in Stratford and confused about her future, if she even wanted one. Her parents had taught her that one's closest loved ones aren't reliable, that love begets hate and the only thing to be achieved in adulthood is a shitty house in Stratford to rot in from the inside out, both figuratively and literally.

She wasn't interested in living that life, in that world. She wanted out and it showed. It showed in her sallow skin and emaciated figure. It showed in her oily hair and unpleasant body odor—the polar opposite to her hygiene now, which explains why she's so obsessed with it. Slowly shrinking away, mentally and physically, she would've died if Frank hadn't discovered her secret.

"Please, just fucking drop it." She sat with her feet on the passenger seat of his truck, her head resting on her knees, her hollow eyes projecting nothing. She wasn't really there.

"Do you even hear yourself, El! Look at me. Look at me!" He grabbed her chin, forcing her to face him.

She raised her eyes drowning in tears. "What?"

"I love you, El. You're all I got, and I can't see you end up like them. We should learn from their mistakes, not repeat them."

She could've just been doing it for attention. Frank was always working or plopped on the couch chugging beers with Clay, watching the game. Frank assumed she was fine because she hadn't cried much since the funeral, that their parents' deaths had been easier on her because of her age. Little did he realize, all she wanted to do was scream her heart out, but she couldn't. Instead, she turned her hatred inward.

That day in his truck, Frank's words seemed to wake her up. "We should learn from their mistakes, not repeat them." She kept repeating the words in her mind, found them comforting, awakening. Future love was suddenly less improbable. She made a promise to herself to find it and fight for it despite her parents. She'd never end up like them. She'd never do what they'd done. Frank's distraught, bloodshot eyes were the color of love. The visible pain on his face, the palpable care for her well-being, reminded her that she was loved. They had each other and were better off on their own.

Years later, when Frank died defending a smaller guy in a bar fight, Ella forgot his comforting words, at least most of the time. Yet she also retained his ability to bounce back. She was determined to make something of herself. She focused on her schooling, made it into NYU's marketing program and began her new life in New York City.

Now she's heading a high-profile, multimillion dollar account at Pure Creative, in a business meeting in Markus's study, in the home of a world famous rapper, and *he's* making *her* a drink. The memory of the vow she made at fifteen and has broken repeatedly over the years pops into her brain the instant she snorts a line of Markus's blow off the top of his purple *Sleeping Beauty* nightstand.

"Ninety-five percent pure yayo," he brags.

She brushes off thoughts of past mistakes, choosing to focus on the present moment. He hands her the drink. "Thanks so much. I don't usually drink dark-colored alcohol. Gives me the absolute worst hangover."

He frowns.

"I mean, special occasion for a special person, am I right? To your birthday!"

He smirks, raising his glass to her, then to his lips. "Thank you, thank you. I think you're pretty special, too."

In minutes, her head begins feeling incredibly heavy, as if she were balancing on it one of those giant baskets that tribal women carry, as she's seen on the *National Geographic* shows when she's hungover and binging Netflix. Whatever's stored in her basket weighs a ton. The room is spinning: first to Markus's platinum records on the walls rotating in place, then back to him laughing maniacally, grabbing his junk. Ella's brain is more junk, and she's losing her balance, the imaginary basket is falling, her head is nodding dramatically. It smacks the corner of the metal bed frame on her way to the ground. The blurry room becomes a pinhole of light, a faraway exit to the cave in her mind. She's gone spelunking. Just before she loses consciousness, she realizes she's been drugged.

While she sleeps, she has a recurring dream of her father. He's a skeleton sitting at the kitchen table in her childhood home, drinking spirits, pouring the dregs down his meatless gullet. The liquid escapes through the spaces in his skeleton, splashing against the little bits of flesh hanging off the bones on its way out. She hears her mother's skeleton cackling from another room in the house. Ella stands by silently. She clears her throat, accidentally getting her father's attention. In a fury, he rises and chases after her. She makes it up the stairs and halfway under her bed before he grabs hold of her legs with skeletal claws, dragging her out. The overwhelming fear of what he's going to do to her usually wakes her up at this moment in the dream, and now is no different.

She gains consciousness face down on Markus's little bed, but this time, the fear in her dreams isn't the only cause. He's ripping off her dress. She hears Sade playing from the speakers in the walls. Feigning unconsciousness and paralysis, she keeps her eyes shut to block the tears from escaping. She'll cry later. Right now, it's time to figure out how to get out of this.

All the moments her brother protected her play across her eyelids. He taught her to be strong, to fight for what and whom she believes in, to stand up for herself, his priceless words carrying well into her adult life. Strolling home from happy hour after work one night in New York, she had to protect herself from a mugger. He gave her a black eye, but she broke his nose and kept her Gucci and cash. A few years later she confronted her old boss about his relentless come-ons, but, regretfully, she never sued him. The survivor of violence, sexual assault and several turbulent love affairs, she's become callous, proud and ambitious, despite how much her anxiety, insecurities and vices have challenged her inner strength.

Markus pulls her dress over the heels of her feet and past her toes and rolls her onto her back. She opens her eyes, locating his face and kicking it with all the strength she can muster. Stunned, he struggles to stand, waving back and forth like one of those inflatable tube men in the parking lot of an auto dealership. She wobbles to her feet, her adrenaline giving her the power to shove him. As her eyes follow him to the floor, she notices the glass tumbler she was holding before she passed out. It's cracked and is on its side in a small dark puddle of the drug-laced liquor. He groans. She grabs the glass. He tries pushing himself up, only to go dizzy and lose his balance.

Collapsing on his back, he scolds himself for doing her when he's drunk. He never would've made such a rookie mistake if he weren't so stressed and exhausted from his birthday and the recent bad press. The need for sexual release was greater than the need to follow the rules. Besides, they're his rules. He made them, so he can change them. But in this moment, he's the half-conscious subservient one. In this moment, Ella is tying his hands behind his back with the zip tie handcuffs he keeps around just in case the girls wake up while he's pounding them on his little bed. But in all the years he's been creating his fantasy of fucking dead girls—if only he could lower their body temperature—Ella is the only one who ever woke up before the length of time he'd estimated it would take. In this moment of being incapacitated in his own home, the utter disrespect for his celebrity status, he sobers with furious eyes.

"You fucking cunt, I'll kill you! Help! White Lexi!... I said fucking Lexi, you fat fucking bitch, get in here!"

"Wow... you weren't lying when you said this room is soundproof."

Ella's tolerance for drugs is helping her resist the effects of Markus's rape cocktail and fight back. It seems all the partying has paid off. She hits him in the temple with the heavy glass, which doesn't break. Fear-fueled anger, dizzying confusion: neither of these intense feelings fully describe everything she's experiencing emotionally right now. She wonders whether the effects of the drugs are tricking her into sensing Frank's presence or if he's really here with her, surrounding her, this little bed. His aura hangs protectively over her, instructing her to fight for her life and the lives of every other woman Markus hurt in the past or will in the future. Two bright red beams of light coming from Ella's eyes are burning holes in his bleeding face. Thoughts continue racing in her throbbing brain, whirring like a dying toy drone, fast and slow, fast and slow. Should she run out or teach him a lesson?

Taking in her blurry surroundings, she has a flashback to reading *Die Softly* as a teen growing up in the nineties. She was obsessed with Christopher Pike's young adult thrillers in which sex, drugs, murder and suicide were celebrated and indulged. The book is about a high school photographer and peeping Tom named Herb, who keeps a camera hidden in the cheerleaders' locker room and captures a photo of a murder-in-progress on it. He becomes paranoid that Alexa, the killer, knows he took the picture and is coming after him. At the end of the book, she gets him in her clutches and murders him so uniquely that it's stuck with Ella all these years. Markus deserves a similar fate, she decides.

As he lies unconscious, breathing deeply, she rummages through the bottom drawer of the nightstand, finding dildos of assorted sizes, a silver spoon, lube... and duct tape. She gets on the bed and saddles Markus, leaning forward to reach his face and seal his mouth shut. She moves on to his cuffed wrists, slowly wrapping the tape around them for extra security, her own hands shaking. Fully awake now, he's wriggling his legs to stop her from taping them too and manages to kick her halfheartedly in the forehead. Dazed but undefeated, she doesn't stop trying. In time he weakens enough for her to get the tape around his ankles.

"You know, I would've put out without all this," she slurs.

A woozy Markus winces from his head wounds.

"How long have you been doing this?"

He ignores her, looking at the headboard, pretending she's not there, that this isn't happening. She's pacing the room like a zombie, debating what to do next, and notices an iPhone on a little tripod behind a potted cactus near the door. It's been recording everything.

"This is too sick. I can't even. The *Holy War* project? *Helping people*? You're just a wolf in sheep's clothing, aren't you?"

He mumbles something inaudible through the duct tape, looking at her for the first time since she brought him down.

"I don't care what you have to say." She sticks the rolled hundred-dollar bill directly in the kilo bag of cocaine, snorting deeply. The boost is nearly immediate, diluting the effects of Markus's cocktail. "Your turn."

Her body calms from the balance of uppers and downers. She picks up the bag of coke and carries it with her onto the bed. Conquering his resisting body by punching his balls repeatedly like she's playing Whack-A-Mole, she mounts him again. He curls up like a fetus. The duct tape muffles his screams. From the bag, she scoops out a handful of coke and brings it under his heaving nostrils. The burning in his nose momentarily distracts him from his swelling genitals.

In the vein of Alexa's method for murdering Herb in *Die Softly*, Ella forces Markus to inhale handful after handful of coke. He has no choice with his mouth taped shut, leaving him his nose to breathe with. It's either oxygen and coke or nothing at all. As much as he tries to stop himself from breathing, his body refuses to cooperate. The two pills of Viagra he took before reaching for her dress, the drinking since eleven a.m. and the overload of cocaine are enough to give him a heart attack, and he has just that. A trickle of vomit pushes through the side of his taped mouth. He begins convulsing, his bugged eyes seemingly popping out of his head. For just a split second, his face morphs into her father's. She physically shakes it off. His eyes roll back in his head and his body goes lifeless. Blood streams from his nostrils down his face.

She screams as loud as she can. She screams till her voice is hoarse. She screams for her adolescent self, for remaining silent when her drunken father began molesting her a year after the three boys had attacked her. To try to bury the pain, she never told anyone about it, not even Frank. During the following hungover mornings, her father would excuse his behavior by claiming he'd confused her with her mother. The one time she tried telling her mother about the abuse, her mother called her a lying homewrecker slut and refused to discuss it further.

Ella picks up her heels from under the bed and puts them on. Immediately she's taller. Her ex, Ian, comes to her racing mind for the first time in a while. She recalls the morning she spiked his smoothie with LSD and unintentionally ended their relationship. He wasn't right for her anyway, she realized soon after. Assholes like Dylan have always been more her speed—or maybe it was his supposed spirituality that reminded her of Frank. She thinks of Frank's best friend Clay, his dead son Bryce. She'll give Clay a ring after this, see how he's doing. Seeing as her life as she knows it will undoubtedly end after tonight, she'll have the time. But for now, she needs to focus.

Suddenly she's in the private bathroom of the study. The overhead light is magnificently bright, like the light some people claim to see during near-death experiences. She looks at herself in the mirror: disheveled hair, makeup smeared across her face like a sad clown, hands shaking something awful.

With the Aesop hand soap sitting on the sink in a dark translucent plastic bottle, she washes her hands and face, smooths back her sweat-soaked hair. Her face reddens as tears come, ready or not. She sobs over the white marble sink. When she's done, she rinses her swollen face and teary bloodshot eyes.

Wearing Markus's oversized, bedazzled Balmain sweatshirt because he tore her dress, she exits much more easily than she thought. His bodyguard Jay half nods when he sees her leaving the study, assuming her bedraggled look is the result of another one of Markus's wild nights. Earlier, Jay heard muffled screaming as he stood watch by the bedroom door. Markus wrecked another girl, lucky him, is what he thought then.

Ella loses her way, ending up in the middle of the party, forced to take the long way out through the intoxicated, pretentious crowd. She feels them eyeing her in the sweatshirt Markus was wearing, wondering where he is. "Skinny little slut," their eyes say. The nearest exit, which she takes, leads into the backyard. White Lexi, who's flirting with a behemoth Black man who may be The Rock, catches Ella escaping.

"Hey girl, meeting over? Did Markus come out with you?"

She freezes in surrender, worrying that White Lexi somehow knows what she did and is about to pounce on her. "No, he's... I mean, he said he wanted to nap."

"Talking business always wears him out."

Ella stands there awkwardly. Lexi notices the signs. Ella wears herself like a rain-soaked jacket hanging limply on a coatrack: arms swaying at her sides, hands trembling, her wide-eyed face slick and drooping. Lexi shrugs off the guilt in her heart.

"The valet is on the other side, but if you don't want to go through the house, you can walk that way around the building."

"Oh... thanks."

An embarrassed, angry and terrified Ella walks away with her proverbial tail between her legs. Reaching the front of the residence, she spots the young Mexican-looking valet in a matte black short bus that's decorated in symmetrical rows of gold string lights. He takes her down the endless driveway with three other guests catching Ubers at the gates. They're all B-list TV actors, two of whom she recognizes from her favorite FX series, none of whom acknowledge her during the ride back. They're immersed in drug-laced banter about upcoming jobs, each trying to one-up the other. Ella doesn't notice their ignoring her. She's in shock from what just happened, what Markus did, what she did, that she may have killed him. Did she really do it, or was the last bit a hallucination? She knows the answer.

The steel-framed gate at the entrance to the property opens gracefully, freeing her at last. Stepping off the bus and just about to order her own Uber, she glances down at the phone she's been clutching in her right hand to the point of crushing it, and realizes it isn't hers. It opens without a password. She remembers now. She used Markus's face to disable the password protection before she left him worse for wear. Only the system default apps display on screen; the phone isn't connected to a network. She opens the photo library, thumbing through dozens of videos of unconscious women and Markus doing his thing to them, *in* them. Despite how horrific they all are, her adolescent-self is granted peace by the one that recorded her night of fighting back, but she wonders whether it was self-defense or revenge.

She thinks of the Pure team, of Link and Brandon—no word from him all day—their CEO Robin and the others, their reactions when they hear the truth about Markus. She'll be the catalyst for the end of the *Holy War* project. Link has been so happy about having this rare opportunity to do something good, despite "the evil, manipulative industry" in which he complains they all work. *Holy War* would've given help and hope for the future to underprivileged people of all ages. Ella was only ever concerned about getting press in *AdAge*, *AdWeek*, major cultural, gossip and fashion magazines, and various news outlets. Showered with accolades that run the gamut—Globes, Cannes Lions, Emmys—the *Holy War* project would've taken Pure from a boutique creative agency to one that rivaled the Wieden+Kennedy's and 72andSunny's of the ad world. Whatever their intent, philanthropic or self-serving, *Holy War* is no longer in the cards for them. Given

Markus's true nature, it wasn't real to begin with. Work is the least of Ella's problems now, anyway.

Without a working phone or the faintest desire to ask one of the drunken guests for help, she slips off her heels and starts walking out of Bel Air. Twenty minutes pass, and she's on Sunset, heading west. She walks and walks, with the occasional car horn assaulting her ears. Thoughts of her phone back in the study and her fears of the future come and pass just like everyone and everything else. What will she do now? What *did* she do? She thinks of her awful parents, their gruesome deaths. Before tonight, she believed she succeeded in not turning into them, but now she's not so sure.

A guy hanging out the passenger side window of a Tesla driving by cheers her on as she vomits on the sidewalk. "Fuck yeah!" All the men she fucked, loved and lost flash before her eyes with each heave of her stomach. Propping herself up against a tree that smells of urine, she catches her breath and gathers her thoughts, remembering the meditation technique Frank taught her to do whenever she was getting anxious.

"Breathe in through your nose and out from your mouth. Take inventory of your body, from your toes to your head." His voice is carried to her ears with the chilly night wind. "Be present... the present is all we have," he whispers audibly.

She continues walking. For hours.

As she makes her way down the last hill before the Pacific Coast Highway, she sees the rising sun's reflection dancing in the breathtaking ocean on the other side of it. Following the pedestrian crossing painted white across the highway, she nears a wrinkle-faced homeless woman leaning against a streetlight. High above their heads, the streetlight's bulb is dimming in the morning sun. The homeless woman is having a heated conversation with no one, holding a rotten apple rind to her ear. Ella stops staring and walks away briskly. Finally, she reaches the glittering water, crying and laughing softly.

CHAPTER NINE

An Influencer
in the Morning

ELIZABETH AKA WHITE LEXI pulls herself up by the back of the white suede sectional. Yawning faintly, she casts disgruntled eyes on the gardener, Edher. He's singing in Spanish with his headphones on, tinkering with the irrigation system in a perfectly manicured yard. There's nothing between her and the outside, nothing to block out his butchering of "Con Altura" by Rosalia.

"You fat fool," she scolds herself, having forgotten to close the retractable glass walls of the mansion before passing out... again. Markus will flip if he sees this.

Last night, fashion legend Barbeau gave Markus a round white clock with "PERMANENT" stamped on its glass front in the familiar Helvetica type and quotations of his street fashion label Dark-White. A drunken Markus made Lexi mount it above the modern gas fireplace at around midnight. She glances up to check the time, instantly panicking because the clock is off-center. The Chanel Guillotine is right over there. She could just end things, but she isn't confident the artist Tom Sachs built it to be functional.

"Edher! Edher!"

He races over.

With hand gestures, speaking slowly, stopping at every syllable, she has him adjust the clock's position.

The maid service is arriving at noon to pick up the remains of last night's shenanigans, which carried well into morning. If Markus's palace isn't pristine by sundown, he'll lose it on her. On top of the stressful workday ahead, she's bloated from the fried pickles and Diet Cokes that fueled her third wind at five a.m. to maintain the bubbly, confident persona he and his friends find so entertaining. One of her fake lashes came unglued while she slept. Neon blue eyeshadow is caked on her dehydrated eyelids, and her clear blue eyes have turned bloodshot behind shriveled contacts. Several drops of the ranch dressing she had with the fried pickles have encrusted on her sequin MSGM bomber jacket—she'll have to send Edher to the dry cleaners.

Deflated black and gold balloons, half-empty bottles and baggies, broken glasses and torn condom wrappers litter Markus's beautiful home. An ice sculpture of him naked— with an inaccurately sized penis—is turning into a puddle on the white marble floor. As much as she loves being his arguably underpaid personal assistant and the perks that come with it, she hates dealing with the cleanup crew after one of his parties, especially his annual birthday extravaganza. He can always afford more help, real help, but he limits his inner circle to the friends and family who were around before he became famous.

White Lexi is a curation of styles and personality traits she's stolen from famous others onscreen and in magazines, and from friends and acquaintances over the years. Markus began calling her White Lexi about a year and a half ago when Lexi the Black pop star rose to fame. Excluding their skin color and hair, they're practically twins: identical spacing between dark green eyes, the same wide nose, round jawline, thick lips, high cheekbones and full figure. Elizabeth only goes by Lexi now. She changed her Instagram handle to @WhiteLexi and has nearly 200,000 followers, but not just because of the name or her being *the* Markus's personal assistant. She's also his cousin, and with an Instagram grid packed with pics of him and his crew, the Night Army, she ensures no one forgets it.

She considers herself the right kind of fat person. She has a gorgeous face, exercises regularly, and is perfectly healthy per the results of her annual physical. Drawn in by the allure of her body-positive posts, her followers "slip into her social" daily like the lyrics in "Facts Sting" by the real Lexi, who turned body acceptance into a trendy movement. A few weeks ago, the real Lexi hugged her in front of the step-and-repeat at Markus's album release party, but she thinks the gesture was all business, as the real Lexi wants to open for his upcoming European tour.

Sitting back on the sofa, thumbing through his Instagram, she counts how many stories she posted as him last night. He/she must've beat Trump in posting the most times in the least number of hours. Granted, Markus's content is visual fun on Instagram versus the president's verbal diarrhea on Twitter—this past winter Trump had hosted him at a White House dinner, followed by a private chat to which White Lexi hadn't been invited.

Last night she also sent Markus's dick pics to one lucky lady and made plans for her to grace the twin-sized bed in his study earlier this morning. The woman should be gone by now. Around two hours into any given good-time girl's stay, his bodyguard Jay knocks on the door, saying he has to leave for an important meeting with his label, regardless of the time of day.

Several months ago, Lexi had cameras installed in the frames of the multi-platinum records hanging in his study. Each camera captures a unique angle of his many sexual es- capades. She doesn't pity the string of mostly blondes he films without their knowledge. If they don't realize what they're getting into when they respond to dick pics and "U up?" texts, that's their problem. They remind her of the sorority girls who spent nearly every Sunday at the gym on Elizabeth's college campus, where she wasted two and a half years of her life feeling constantly rejected. Running off their hangovers on treadmills, followed by commiserating in the cafeteria over late night hookups at whatever frat party they'd attended the night before, the sorority girls would be genuinely confused why the guys hadn't replied to their texts yet.

"Maybe I'm getting fat! I can't believe I ate *two* sweet potato fries and a *whole handful* of dark chocolate M&M's in the caf. And there was nothing skinny about those margaritas. We're talking a hundred calories... *each.*"

"Oh my god, I know. I was so fit yesterday, and now I'm just like this bloated beluga."

"We're running ninety minutes today."

"Minimum."

Nowadays, Elizabeth-turned-White-Lexi follows a strict beauty regimen herself: morning run, Pilates and exfoliation, makeup touchups every four to six hours, nightly microdermabrasion, monthly vampire facials, skincare by La Mer, lasers and preventative injectables as needed, all with the trust fund her grandfather left her to foot the bills. Besides Markus, she doesn't communicate with the rest of her self-involved family. Other than hunger, fatigue, boredom and the associated relief she gets from eating, sleeping, fucking, not to mention the attention from posting raunchy photos on Instagram, she feels and wants for little else.

Perhaps her lack of empathy for Markus's girls stems from the bullying she endured as a kid. In middle school, her classmates exchanged fat jokes just a row or two behind her as if she couldn't hear their careless whispers. When she began wearing more fashionable clothes in high school, they retaliated with insults about her fitted outfits, claiming that a girl with her figure shouldn't be squeezing into such clothing. At USC, she ran every morning, including weekends, lost a few pounds and gained some confidence. She dared to show her face at a frat party one crisp fall evening. An anonymous someone in the drunken crowd shouted, "Hey Hog Jogger!" They all crowed with laugher like it was the smartest joke in the world, too intoxicated to bother hiding their disgust for her as they usually had. She laughed at herself too, a high-pitched cackle she'd reserved for such mortifying moments.

The tables turned when Elizabeth dropped out of school to ride the coattails of Markus's success. To this day, random classmates emerge from the woodwork a few times a month, attempting to reminisce over their supposed friendships in high school and at college. Lexi loves seeing recent pics of the sorority girls who've lost their looks and gotten fat. Some of them are still living with their parents. A few are strapped with kids and hideous husbands with menial jobs while she lives the life of a rap star.

Lexi sighs, entering the nearest bathroom, which is in utter ruins: walls smeared with lipstick, wine-stained tiles, a used condom half filled with goo on a bed of bloody and brown tissues in a gold-plated trashcan. She walks to a marble sink caked in vomit. Someone appears to have tried draining the mess but clearly failed. Breathing through her mouth to avoid the stench, she examines herself in the mirrored wall behind the sink. Her eyes are puffy, curls crooked. She splashes cold water on her face, slightly improving her appearance but not enough to be seen in public, let alone by Markus. Throwing on her favorite Sunday Service hoodie by Kanye West, a pair of oversized Celine sunglasses and the soiled sequin jacket, she reapplies hot pink lipstick, smacks her lips in the mirror and makes her way down to the study.

She knocks on the door, inadvertently pushing it open. Strange, she thinks. Markus gets more paranoid when he's partying, so the deadbolt is usually locked the day following one of his bashes.

"Markus, baby, you alive in there?" An LED table lamp spotlights a big bag of coke on the purple nightstand. Lexi notices something moving, hears a plastic bag rustling. She removes her sunglasses, sees Jay the bodyguard. He's sweaty, his brow furrowed, and he has dark stains on his black pants and T-shirt—odd because he only ever wears the black Prada suit and tie, per Markus's orders. "What you doing in here? You the maid now?" she says.

"I came to check on him. He hadn't come out since that girl."

"Let me get the overhead light, can't see shit," she says, feeling for the switch on the wall.

"Leave it off, Elizabeth. Just get the fuck out. Wait ten minutes, then call 911."

Her vision adjusts to the dark room. Everything seems in order except for the unnatural silence and Jay standing there like a serial killer, clutching a black garbage bag. He's glowering in front of the twin-sized bed, using his colossal figure to block her view. It's the only place to sit other than Markus's custom-made office chair from Herman Miller—whenever he has late visitors, he'll snag the chair, so the cramped bed is the only seat available.

Jay the bodyguard, Jay the fixer, the only one in Markus's crew who isn't family or a pre-fame friend. He's always made Lexi nervous, but she figures that's part of his job description. Fixers like the one in *Ray Donovan* and The Wolf in *Pulp Fiction* have come across just as weird and intimidating. But Jay's clenched jaw and foreboding look are worse than usual. Something is terribly wrong. She nods without another word, backing out of the study. As she moves, she gets a better view of the room, with the light from the hallway reflecting off her sequin jacket, illuminating Markus splayed across the bed. A piece of silver tape is hanging from his mouth. His head rests in vomit. This unnatural version of her cousin paired with Jay's threatening presence propels her down the hall and out the front door faster than she ever ran at college.

"Elizabeth!" Jay shouts but doesn't go after her.

She races to Edher in the backyard. He's dancing to the music playing from his matte red Beats Solo Pro head-phones—he's barely taken them off since Markus gave them to him last Christmas. Clipping the hedges into animal silhou-ettes à la Edward Scissorhands, as an automatic lawn mower tends to the lush grass—despite the drought—he doesn't im-mediately notice her.

"Edher!" she hollers, waving her arms in his face.

"Si?"

"Do you have your phone? It's Markus, we need to call an ambulance!"

"No entiendo, no entiendo."

"Phone! Fucking phone!" She brings her right pinky and thumb to her ear to mimic a phone.

He pulls a filthy flip phone from the stained chest pocket of his white Hanes T-shirt, doing his best to hide the animosity he has for her. She's never treated him with even an ounce of respect. He isn't as bothered when Markus does it because he's a huge celebrity and signs his paychecks. But Lexi always makes him do work outside of gardening, like cleaning her pigsty of a Tesla, fetching a Diet Coke on the rocks while her fat ass lazes on a pool chair, or hanging a clock like he's some *maricón* interior decorator.

Snatching the phone from him like he stole it from her, she dials 911 with clammy thumbs, ignoring Jay's order to wait ten minutes before calling for help. "Get me an ambulance now! This is Markus we're talking about, *the* Markus!" she shouts while pacing the virtually endless backyard.

She trips over the robotic lawn mower, the phone flies out of her hand, and she lands flat on her face. An amused Edher relishes the moment for a few seconds before running over to help her, feigning concern.

"Señora! Señora!"

"Ma'am? Hello? Ma'am. Ma'am, can you tell me Markus's last name?" the 911 operator implores.

Lexi, dazed, doesn't hear either of them.

CHAPTER TEN

Influencers in the Afternoon

WHITE LEXI TAPS HELP, then Help Center, then Managing Your Account, then Delete Your Account. Instead of erasing her social media presence for good, she *could* just delete Instagram from her phone until the scandal dies down. But that's just wishful thinking, isn't it? The videos are so viral, there should be a new word to describe the rapid spread of their disease. She's getting just as many DMs and emails as usual, but they're not from old classmates turned frenemies trying to reconnect or dudes trying to get it in. They're from major tabloids and Markus's angry fans.

The major tabloids ask, "Were you aware?"

The angry fans say, "She must've known."

Yes, she was, and yes, she did... to an extent.

Some of Markus's victims maintain she was the orchestrator. She should die. Fat ugly bitch. Lexi wannabe. The mean comments below her Instagram posts go on and on. Even the real popstar Lexi posted her own Instagram Story with White

Lexi's username tagged. "Take my name out your handle, get your ass to jail and bring the Night Army wit you #lockthemup!"

According to an article in the *Times*, a confidential source close to the police investigation told the paper that she and Markus's crew, the Night Army, were being investigated for aiding Markus in at least three of the sexual assaults. That is, except for the virtuous Baby, Markus's DJ and business manager, whose innocence is in line with his nickname. Also, Baby and his TV star girlfriend just announced that she's pregnant, again. After the last two miscarriages they're praying every minute that this one keeps. He hasn't called White Lexi or replied to her texts since the Markus incident. Considering he publicly denounced Markus's actions and resigned from the Night Army, she isn't at all surprised.

Shortly after the news broke about Markus's girls, Telco canceled the *Holy War* project, citing a breach of contract—which had never actually been countersigned by Markus—specifically the morality clause. "Markus's actions are the antithesis of Telco's core values as a brand and what we aim to achieve with our corporate social responsibility initiatives for which we invest upward of $4B per year. The series we've been developing in partnership with Markus, which was intended to aid the disadvantaged, won't be moving forward given the tragic and criminal nature of its originator. Our hearts go out to all of Markus's victims and their families."

For the last two weeks, a humiliated and defeated Lexi hasn't left Markus's guest house to keep up with her beauty regimen. Her visit to him in the hospital was a media nightmare, so she won't be going back there either. Anyway, it's not like he knew she was there. She used to bask in the public's all-eyes-on-her, but now she's terrified of the aggressive paparazzi, the confrontational reporters and Markus's disgruntled fans. Flinging her phone to the floor, she flops on the bed face first. Her sheets smell ripe. Where's Edher the gardener when she needs him to help her tidy? Oddly enough, he was the first to quit, despite how much she thought he loved working for them.

The last bit of help Markus employed regularly quit after Edher had. Markus and Lexi considered him the most trusted and devoted employee of the house. He claimed to be leaving because he was worried about the negative attention from the LAPD, that it'd somehow lead to his deportation. Lexi's days by the Olympic-sized swimming pool with him at her service are gone forever. The manicured landscaping has been neglected, becoming messy and overgrown, just like her. There's no one left to comfort her. Her family has all but disowned her, and Markus's parents haven't returned her calls or emails, nor have they made a public statement in their son's defense or otherwise. She's truly, utterly, alone.

She regrets her insincerity in the thinly remorseful, final Instagram message about her unknowing involvement in Markus's crimes, which she posted with a closeup pic of her crying eyes. "If I had known I was ushering his lady friends to the slaughter rather than a consensual sexual encounter, as Markus had led me to believe, I'd have never gone along with it. I'm just as much of a victim here!"

Markus's lawyers have advised her to remain silent, but she had to at least try to redeem herself in the public eye. In truth, she's just sad that the fun of fame is over. She's always known that Markus took advantage of his young admirers, but his actions were pretty vanilla for male A-listers, at least the dozens she knows. The leaked recordings tell a much darker story. Whether or not they're authentic, his lavish life of celebration is dead, so he should stay in his coma. When— if—he wakes up, his next bed will be a hard one in prison, she expects. Vegetation or death are better options.

Despite the fallout, money won't be an issue, thanks to her trust fund. But where can she go? She's infamous, confined to Markus's property. The dramatic physical transformation of pop star Adele comes to mind. If Lexi has her stomach stapled and hair cut and colored, she'll be able to venture outside un-spooked—if the police don't arrest her first.

More than anything, she's furious at that good-time girl Ella, a nobody who would've remained basic and unnamed like the rest of Markus's whores if she hadn't posted those videos, including the one of Ella herself. She's just as guilty as Lexi for all the things she did to Markus, but the police don't seem too focused on Ella's case since finding her in some shitty town in Connecticut. They're holding her for questioning, but she has yet to be officially charged. She's practically being celebrated in the press like she's the face of the MeToo movement, a victim-turned-heroine who fought to save herself and punish a sexual predator at the height of his fame, while Lexi is stuck inside like she's on house arrest, hated by herself and others, completely ashamed of her present social status. Sighing, she ruminates over her unpromising future. She just can't go back to being Elizabeth, not after the safety of White Lexi, of being the cousin of *the* Markus. Each day she realizes more and more that there's nothing left for her. She'll always be the sad lonely girl with a weight problem whom nobody wants.

Part of her hates Markus almost as much as Ella, not to mention herself when she was Elizabeth, just another friendless fat girl. When she saw the videos, she had a flashback to a keg party in their high school years. Markus threw the bash in the woods behind his house when his parents were out of town. At some point that night she blacked out, woke up in pain, her panties bloody. She had no recollection of who'd taken her virginity, but she knew it was gone. Finding comfort in Markus's arms, she cried her eyes out, never suspecting it'd been him.

In two-day-old undies and no bra, she slides off the bed. Approaching with great reluctance an ornately framed full-length mirror, she examines the results of her recent inactivity and lack of hygiene. Her blond curls have gone from bouncy and beaming to tangled and greasy. Without her morning routine of a Runyon Canyon run and personal Pilates session, her figure has gone from svelte and voluptuous to saggy and jiggly. Everything hangs from her bones like fat-laden meat on a spit, ready to be cooked over a blazing fire. A shiny T-zone peppered with oversized blackheads has overtaken her clear, iridescent complexion.

Tears arrive unexpectedly. Her chubby face reddens and swells like a puffer fish. She finds herself missing the swarm of cops who searched the mansion for the last two weeks. Detective Sorenson, a tall, handsome older man channeling Jeremy Irons, was flirting with her during the search, but when she texted something sexually suggestive to the number on his business card, he told her he was married and even if he were single, he'd never fraternize with a suspected accomplice to rape—later he scolded himself for his unprofessional response, but his daughter is a survivor of an unsolved rape, so he couldn't help himself.

Lexi is disgusted with her reflection in the mirror and her bitch-ass emotional outburst. She wipes her tears. Sucking in her stomach and covering the rest of her body with strategically placed arms, she feels a bit better about herself. A lightbulb of an idea switches on in her head. She's ready to shed her old skin and undergo another reinvention. Inside the fragile cocoon that is White Lexi someone new and alive is a cookin'…

Over the last year or so since the sordid videos had gone public, Detective Sorenson has brought Lexi in for questioning six times. On each occasion, she's stuck with the same story. She doesn't know anything, she's just as appalled and as much of a victim as the girls in those videos. He's ended each interrogation on the same note. "We'll be in touch. As a reminder, you're restricted from leaving California while the investigation is ongoing."

During their last meeting, she shared the memory of the keg party, her voice breaking as she revealed that Markus had raped her too. Sorenson could see she was telling the truth—he knows the signs all too well. He wasn't as convinced that she and the Night Army had nothing to do with procuring Markus's girls. There were too many statements from witnesses—most of which the district attorney considers hearsay, true as they may be.

Much earlier in the investigation, Sorenson's tech team combed through every video of the assaults that Markus had recorded with hidden cameras in his study, every text on his phone, her own, and the stockpile of hard drives and other iPhones they found in his wall safe. The videos provided enough proof to lock up Markus for two lifetimes but lacked any evidence that would implicate Lexi. Still, Sorenson's gut tells him that she's culpable in some way, and it's only a matter of time till he finds proof of her involvement—detective work is a waiting game, and he always plays to win.

Her text replies to Markus's demands were consistently acquiescent, always cautious, forever apologetic, which, Sorenson has deduced, further implies that she was helping Markus lure in his unsuspecting victims.

"I'm craving that duck from Daniel in NYC, call the restaurant and have it flown here by tomorrow."

"On it, boss," she replied.

"Remember that shirt I saw at that store on tour? I want three."

"Do you remember the brand? Never mind, I'll figure it out."

"I'm hungover, the IV isn't working, and I need a cure by the show tonight. Do your fucking job and fix me!"

"Oh no! I'll get a doctor here within the hour."

If anything is clear, it's that she never wanted to disappoint her cousin, her boss, the benefactor of her own small fame, her Svengali since childhood. Sorenson learned even more about her past from the former sorority girls with whom she'd gone to college. They came forward on their own, hoping for their own fifteen minutes in front of the cameras outside the police station. Sure, Lexi's PTSD from being bullied in school and raped by Markus primed her for extreme subservience and various identity crises, but Sorenson's sympathy for her has been overshadowed by her despicable actions.

On the flip side, Lexi's worrying over getting arrested has dissipated over time. If the police were going to snatch her up, they'd have done so by now—it's been a year! Every "business meeting" that she orchestrated on Markus's behalf was coordinated on his phone. The police found nothing on her mobile device or her personal and business computers except for an infinite number of dictatorial messages from Markus. Hearing them read back to her all at once—and more than once—during the countless police interrogations she's suffered through, she's come to realize that her White Lexi persona has been nothing more than a pseudo-famous, obedient fatty dying to fit in. It's high time she leaves her second self in the back of her mind, on the shelf beside Elizabeth, where she'll collect dust for infinity.

Lexi's stylist, Bash, is doing her hair in the privacy of Markus's pool house. He finds it strange that a twenty-nine-year-old wants to dye her naturally blond curls jet black and get a permanent like it's 1981, but he wasn't about to turn down two grand. He took an Uber to the property instead of his own car. In oversized Tom Ford sunglasses and a black vintage hoodie from the days of American Apparel, he's concealed his identity from the paparazzi, who've been stalking the mansion again.

Two weeks ago, a little over a year after Ella had put him in a coma, Markus croaked in the hospital, disgraced, alone, and handcuffed to his bed. Three days after he'd died, his lawyers served Lexi with an eviction notice. Her aunt and uncle inherited everything, and they want her off the property within the next thirty days. If she refuses to go willingly, they're prepared to have the police remove her. She didn't attend the wake or the funeral, fearing public exposure would derail her plans of reinvention. She also didn't want to see Markus's parents, let alone her own—if they were even able to pause their seemingly endless holiday to send off their dead nephew.

After Bash does his magic and leaves, Lexi examines herself in a mirrored wall of the master bedroom in the main house—she made Markus's room her own—which she's been reduced to cleaning herself. With the color and perm, the afro hair clip-ins for extra body, and her tanning by the dirty pool under the scorching spring sun—drinking warm Diet Cokes she has to get herself—she's confident that her transformation from White Lexi into a brand-new someone is nearing completion.

"Hi, I'm Liz…"

"What up, I'm Liz…"

"Yo, what's good? Liz here."

She empathizes with transsexuals, who are compelled to fix the bodies they were assigned at birth. Nature makes mistakes, too. She's reminded of this whenever she looks at her chubby face in the mirror, every sleepless night she spends pinching her belly fat while staring at the increasingly cobwebbed ceiling above her bed. The shadows of the girls whom she helped Markus hurt dance above her till sunrise. By morning she forgets them, but the sky inevitably turns black again and they rise once more.

Well before she introduced her disgraced alter ego White Lexi to the world, Elizabeth had already been a pop star in her mind, the *real* Lexi, among other remarkable personas. She'd just needed a way to express herself, to show the world what she was really made of. For all of Markus's faults, what he'd done to her in their teens, and later, how he treated her as his assistant, he saved her from herself. In a way, she'll always be grateful.

But his death begot her own demise. The public killed her second self just as they had him, so she must reinvent herself again or get in the ground too. Where fame and fortune once took precedence, she's decided to slot in her newfound passion for activism, specifically Black rights and police reform. Inspired by Jonathan Bachman's iconic 2016 photograph *Taking a Stand in Baton Rouge*, in which a young Black woman with her arms crossed resolutely confronts a line of police in riot gear, Lexi's third self materializes as a Black activist named Liz Arnold.

With the Black Lives Matter protests spreading around the world as rapidly as COVID-19, the paparazzi at the gates have begun to thin. Photos of countrywide riots, news of dead innocents and rising cases of the virus have been prioritized over celebrity gossip.

Liz calls Bash a few weeks after he did her hair. He's the only person she's been in touch with for months, so she feels comfortable asking him for a ride to the protests in Santa

Monica—yesterday her aunt had Markus's luxury car collection towed, including the Tesla Liz had been driving. Plus, Bash is an ally for the cause, at least based on his recent Instagram Stories in which he's marching the streets of L.A. to honor George Floyd and Breonna Taylor, calling for the defunding of police.

In his usual oversized black-on-black clothes, Bash arrives in his own car this time, a black 2020 Chevy Blazer with all the fixings. With the car windows down and his shiny, dirty blond hair fluttering in the wind, it's clear that he's less concerned about being seen in public with her. The unbearable boredom of living in a city closed for business during the pandemic trumps the threat of bad press. If anything, he finds it amusing and ridiculous, especially the hair makeover—and she's calling herself Liz now?

The hangover he had this morning has begun to ease with the help of a blunt and two Adderall. At an over-capacity illegal house party last night, he bragged about his plans to protest the police with the new and improved White Lexi. The bash took place at an influencer mansion in the Hills that his gay-famous drag queen friends have been renting. They've been livestreaming their debauchery on OnlyFans every weekend since Governor Newsom shut down nightclubs—later the governor will shut off their water and electricity for their defying L.A. county's temporary restrictions on social gatherings.

The gates open. He drives slowly up the snaking driveway, finding Lexi—er, Liz—standing proudly in front of Markus's overwhelmingly gorgeous home. The surrounding trees waving in the Santa Ana winds reflect in the exterior glass walls of the mansion behind her. He still gets butterflies at his celebrity clients' dream homes. As much as he's used to interacting with these half-and-half gods, gaining their superficial confidence while doing their hair, he knows he isn't one of them and never will be. He's had his own success and mini fame as a hairstylist to the stars, but he can't help feeling somewhat inferior, even to Lexi/Liz. The closer he gets to his clients, the more he's reminded that he's nothing more than glorified help and a cognitive therapist for the rich and famous. At least the pay is good, he convinces himself.

"Hey, you!"

"Hi, baby."

"Look at you!"

With a black afro, giant gold bangles pulling down her earlobes, dark spray tan and no makeup, she's almost unrecognizable. "You like?" Even her voice is different, deeper. She does a model's spin, showing off the extra pounds she's put on over the last three or four weeks. "Hah ha!"

"*Yass.* You look so..."

"Black?"

"Yes! And even more like the other Lexi. It's uncanny... but um... can I ask why?"

She shrugs, picking up a weekend bag and slinging it over her shoulder. "I just can't be recognized out there. And I'm part Black anyway, so don't give me any cultural appropriation crap. I'm representing my people today."

He remembers the whole scandal surrounding Markus's false claim that he was part Black on his father's side. Someone leaked his birth certificate, proving otherwise. Liz's mom is his father's sister, so Bash knows she's not Black either. But by the frenzied look in Liz's eyes, he senses she needs his acceptance. "Oh, right, well good for you."

"Are we ready to tell the police to stop-shoo-ting-us?" she says like Eva Longoria's "hy-a-lur-on-ic acid" line in those L'Oréal commercials in which she emphasizes each syllable with a clap.

"You're ready to go already? Thought you wanted to smoke first?"

"I meant on the way. This place is a hot mess... they're kicking me out by the way."

"Yeah, you told me," he says, mildly disappointed that they're not staying. He's only seen inside the guest house. "Have you started looking?"

She tosses her bag through the open backseat window of his car—what could she possibly be bringing with her? "Not yet, I've been so busy working on my new look. And the only thing that matters right now—other than getting this goddamn pandemic under control—is the BLM movement."

"Yes, mama, it's important, but you should also sort your livi—"

"I have time. It's all good, baby."

"If you need a good realtor, I do the hair of one of the brokers in the Oppenheimer Group. You know, from the Netflix series *Selling Sunset?*"

"Stop. I love that show. Christine is a badass bitch."

"Girl, yes. I haven't met her, but she seems like a blast."

"We'll see... I've been stuck up in this bitch since well before the pandemic hit. This is my home, so it's not as simple as just packing up and leaving. If these protests weren't so personal, I wouldn't be going anywhere right now. Not trying to catch the plague."

"I hear you, miss thing. Should we get going?"

They hop in the car and drive off. Liz plays Megan Thee Stallion on Apple CarPlay, twerking out of her seat like they're heading to Coachella.

As they're driving into Santa Monica, Bash sees unexplained piles of bricks at major intersections. Like a UFO the mere presence of them provokes curiosity and a sensing of danger. Bash remembers a news article about the anonymous anarchists who've been dropping off the bricks to encourage protestors to riot and loot, but he decides not to mention it. She doesn't notice them anyway because she's too busy ogling herself in the passenger-side rearview mirror.

The closer they get to the action the harder it is to find parking. Giving up, Bash turns back and finds a spot several blocks away. A manic Liz puts on a sparkly rhinestone BLM face mask and grabs her bag from the backseat.

"What you got in there?"

"Just a few things… *gots* to be prepared."

Remnants of American unrest litter their walk to the march: obliterated storefronts and defaced buildings, fresh blood stains in the concrete, the blackened carcass of a burned-out Audi, and a pile of what appears to be human shit on a sidewalk near the Third Street Promenade. They're close to Bash's favorite touristy restaurant, The Misfit—he finds their gluten-free green chili mac and cheese to be simply divine. Sadly, they're closed indefinitely, likely from extended restrictions on public dining.

The stone-faced police with tear gas at the ready, hiding like cowards behind their riot shields, juxtaposed with the roiling crowd of all colors, collide with a beautiful midsummer day, a smiley-face sun and a clear, cornflower-blue sky. The cops are prepared for another battle, the protesters having progressed from peaceful to violent as the day has worn on. Nearby in Venice, looters have destroyed stores by the dozens and are making their way back to Santa Monica for the third night in a row.

"I don't know if this is such a good idea, Le—Liz. The curfew goes into effect in an hour, and those cops don't look like they're messing around."

"Oh my god, chill, don't be such a pussy."

Three news helicopters are circling the scene, anticipating the rioters' clashing with police. Liz slips her heavy bag off her shoulder. Half expecting her to pull out a weapon of some kind, Bash is relieved that it's just a bottle of water, a hairbrush and a toiletry kit. Sitting on the corner she teases out her makeshift afro and pats her greasy brow with an oil-absorbing sheet. Satisfied with the touchups, she throws everything back into the bag. Fishing around the bottom of it she eventually reveals a red rose wrapped in crinkled plastic. She looks up at the choppers, at the nearing crowd down the street and the robotic cops clutching wartime tools before her.

"Liz..."

"Liz..."

"Lexi!"

"What, Bash! What?"

"I think we should get out of here."

"Can you just record this first? Here, take my phone."

"What are you even doing?"

"Fuck man, I'll pay you, just do it."

The unpleasant reminder that he's the help hits him like a brick. That, and a second wave of his hangover. The pills and weed are wearing off. "I'm going."

"Fine. Fuck off with the rest of them."

Bash darts out of sight after she snatches her phone from his hand and positions it against the curb, directing it at the cops and tapping the record button. The phone's camera won't capture her best angles, but she's not that concerned given that the choppers are also documenting everything, as are the photojournalists and unruly protestors in the streets.

A beaming Liz approaches the defensive police, clutching the thorny stem of the rose with two hands, wearing an almost angelic smile that the cops read as crazy.

"Back up, lady. Back. Up. Don't come any closer!"

Thorns pierce her palms, but she keeps progressing as the mob rushes up behind her.

Protestors scream.

Cops shout.

Batons swing.

Bricks fly.

Tear gas envelops the crowd and their cacophonous chanting and everything breaking around them.

Something or someone knocks Liz unconscious.

The next day, Liz's face is on the cover of *The New York Times* and nonstop on CNN, her new name on tongues around the world. She's famous again but in a way that matters. From her hospital bed, with her head neatly bandaged and an extra layer of dark foundation substituting as blackface for her fading spray tan, she takes questions from reporters. She explains to the masses what it feels like to be a Black woman accosted by police while exercising her constitutional right to protest peacefully.

An unemployed Baby offers to help manage the virtually nonstop interview requests coming in, as well as the invites to speaking events centered around the movement, and to pen pieces on her traumatic experience for *Newsweek* and *Time*. The rising star of Liz Arnold the Black activist is the perfect project for someone with his entertainment background. His baby boy was born last year and is in perfect health, so he's ready to get back to work. Plus, the show in which his wife starred was recently canceled, which will give her plenty of free time to raise their son solo—with a little help from her personal assistant and their live-in nanny, of course.

Liz and Baby go on a tour of the protests. Fancying herself the Angela Davis for the new millennium, she rewrites Davis's famous speeches, changing the context to current events. She even plagiarizes the one that Davis delivered at the Embassy Auditorium in Los Angeles in 1972 on behalf of the Soledad brothers, the trio of Black prisoners who'd been wrongly accused of murdering a guard and whom Davis argued were being singled out for voicing their political views and trying to organize other prisoners. In Liz's version of the speech, she changes Davis's call for structural changes within the prison system in the seventies to revamping the police force today.

Rumors of Liz running for senator in California ring true. Baby leads a multi-county operation for her election campaign, its slogan "Liz Arnold, a Black Rose from the Asphalt" alluding to the iconic photo of her confronting police with a

rose in her hands. Pre-election forecasts swing well in her favor. Winning a seat in the Senate seems all but certain.

Liz's memories of Markus and White Lexi fade dramatically as her success progresses. All her actions as Liz have
vindicated her of White Lexi's sins, even if no one other than
Baby knows whom she used to be. She'll live out her days
fighting the good fight for her people, basking in the adora-
tion for her magnanimous public service. It was all worth it.

Waking from her improbable dream isn't as rewarding. During the Santa Monica protests, a rioter recognized Liz as
White Lexi in blackface and hit her in the head with a brick.
For nearly a week since then she's been hospitalized, in a
coma, fantasizing about a happy life she'll never have. A
skinny blond nurse wakes Liz when she drops a glass vase of
flowers from Bash on the floor, the room otherwise devoid of
any get well soon gifts.

The first things Liz sees when she opens her eyes: her right
wrist handcuffed to a cold metal rail alongside the hospital
bed, the uncomfortable plastic tubes in her arm, broken glass
on the floor twinkling in sunlight shooting through dusty
blinds, and the nurse taunting her with her skinny figure.
"Look who's awake! I'll get the doctors."

Liz is too weak to reply or ask why she's tied up. The nurse
doesn't tell her about the side-by-side photos of White Lexi
and Liz headlining the news. "White Lexi, Markus's Alleged
Accomplice, Dons Blackface in Tone-Deaf Publicity Stunt."

On top of the bad press that came out as Liz slept, an organized group of women whom Markus had assaulted made statements about White Lexi's grooming them, and provided saved voicemails and emails proving their claims. Their fears of coming forward died with Markus. He may have gotten off easily, but Lexi is still very much alive to face the music. As the nurse exits, she tells the sleepy cop at the door that Liz is awake.

In a dark blue polo shirt and black chinos, with his badge clipped to a cracked leather belt, Detective Sorenson enters Liz's hospital room less than an hour after the cop texted him. Just as she's beginning to doze again, the tapping sound of his leather-soled cowboy boots on the linoleum floor keeps her awake. She opens her eyes to the handsome man hovering over her with a confident look of accomplishment on his appealing—albeit aging—face, the detective who investigated Lexi's crimes and rejected her sexual advances.

"Ms. Arnold. It's been a while."

Even if she had the strength to speak, she wouldn't have much to say. She knows what his presence means and why she's handcuffed. It's all over for Lexi, for her. The rhythmic beeping of the machines to which she's connected reminds her of how Markus's hit song "Holy War" starts, of how glamorous her life was, and all the things and people she took for granted and hurt to get ahead. She thinks of the girls—the women—who suffered just because she wanted to keep

Markus happy. She's tired of running away from herself, of assuming any persona other than Elizabeth, a stranger.

Seeing how weak she is, Sorenson decides to hold off questioning her. "I'll let you rest. We'll talk when you're better. In the meantime, I advise you to seek legal counsel before you're discharged and in police custody."

A single tear trickles down her cheek, like a bad actor who's making herself cry with a menthol tear stick. He doesn't console her, nor does he care to wonder whether her emotions are genuine. Walking backward toward the door, he eyes her with nothing but disgust. Just before he turns into the hallway, Elizabeth mouths something inaudible. He thinks it may have been "I'm sorry."

CHAPTER ELEVEN

The Kalifornian

A WHIFF OF A RIPE HOMELESS WOMAN passing Link on the street can wholly transport him to the pungent room in which his mother lay dying of breast cancer. The moldy old clothes stench in a consignment shop can take him back to the boarding schools to which his father had shipped him before settling on Breakneck Military Academy. Scents that trigger Link's buried past renew his gratitude for the present, helping him recall the rough childhood that made a man out of him. It's no wonder he's been so worried about catching COVID-19, of the virus killing his sense of smell and inadvertent motivational technique.

More than a year after the *Holy War* project had ended and just a couple months following Markus's death and Lexi's subsequent arrest, Link is enjoying another relaxing weekend alone in his newly rented home in Venice Beach, a bungalow steps from the ocean and as far away from his wife Erica as he can physically be in this country. The solitude has been cathartic so far. After a seemingly endless time stuck with her in their luxury Manhattan apartment while they waited out the statewide lockdown to prevent the spread of the virus, he needed the space.

During their last few months together in New York, all their previously ignored issues festered and multiplied. Without their maid to tidy the tornado that is Erica—clothes, dishes, and don't get him started on the bathroom sink—she went from endearingly messy to disgustingly slobby, leaving him no choice but to clean up after her with growing resentment. Her underlying prejudice against Asians went from mild and half joking to extremely offensive—she's always been a bit of a semi-racist snob, but her tasteless comments were no longer so easy to ignore. The TV was constantly tuned to CNN's coverage of the pandemic. She'd watch it while berating the Chinese in unoriginal slurs "for what they did to our economy." She couldn't get her hair colored or Botox injected. She had to administer her own mani/pedis. Every outfit she bought online while Fifth Avenue remained closed didn't fit to her liking. Despite her gaining a few pounds—they'd both put on a few—Link would've found her sexy dressed in a garbage bag. But she never wanted to have sex anymore because she thought she was ugly and fat. Soon he didn't want it anymore either, instead resigning himself to self-relief in the bathroom.

Without consulting her, he accepted a promotion to head of creative for Pure Creative's burgeoning business in L.A.—

a blatant act of animosity because she'd recently had an abortion behind his back. Sure, she'd hinted at not wanting kids before, but he'd always trumped it up to her youth and vanity, convincing himself that she'd change her mind down the road. As someone who'd grown up in a disjointed family, he'd taken her killing their future as a major blow to his life goals. Since his teen years, he'd been dreaming of marrying and making babies, of growing old as he watched those babies make babies, of floating up to heaven while a slew of blood relatives and his lovely wife for fifty-some-odd years mourned him at his funeral. Erica confessed she wanted none of that. "I'm just not the mothering kind." She only needed dogs, long holidays, and to acquire several homes around the world. He felt like he was suddenly living with a stranger, disappointed in himself for missing all this before they'd made their vows.

She just hadn't learned the trade from her distant mother who'd often dump her with the nanny to go on extended weekend getaways with girlfriends—other trophy wives—to destinations such as Montenegro or Acapulco. The only true parenting Erica had experienced had been with her nanny, but she'd been paid for her services.

Erica didn't speak to Link for the two weeks that followed his accepting the job offer. She felt utterly betrayed that he'd made the decision without her, while completely dismissing his argument that her aborting their love child in secret was much worse. But soon she grew excited about living in a different city after months of isolation, a new home to decorate, bountiful mountains and picturesque beaches to enjoy, warm-weather wardrobe to buy for brunches at Little Beach House in Malibu. It didn't seem to be about wanting to be there with him. Rather, she just needed fresh stimulation.

They agreed that he'd move to L.A. during the summer, despite pandemic-related travel constraints, and she'd come in the fall after showing face at two late August weddings in the Hamptons that had been rescheduled due to the pandemic—designer masks and monogrammed bottles of Purell would be placed at every table setting to help limit the spread of the virus. To avoid raising eyebrows in Erica's social circle, Link's absences would be chalked up to COVID-related restrictions on the maximum number of guests allowed at large gatherings.

A couple weeks before his departure, as boxes of his things piled up around them and long-distance movers arrived to collect it all, she cried virtually nonstop over how much she'd miss him. Fantasies of divorce were consuming his thoughts, so he didn't feel the same. But he replied otherwise.

Fatigued by the tragedy of coronavirus and the false impression that it was dissipating for good, America's focus had shifted—virtually overnight—to that of defunding the police and fighting systemic racism. Erica turned off CNN after it had begun de-prioritizing news about the pandemic over that of global protests calling for the arrests of the cops who'd killed George Floyd and Breonna Taylor. All she had to say about the subject was that she didn't know what to say and that parroting the expected sentiments on social media just because everyone else had been doing it felt disingenuous. "Sure, the whole thing is sad, but what can I do about it?"

Link's attempt to school her on the many ways they could help—donating to the victims' families, calling district attorneys, educating her overly privileged Republican family—was met with one-word answers or a subject change. But when Instagram flooded everyone's feeds with information on how to support the movement and how staying silent was considered just as bad as siding with the racists, she went from perfectly speechless to obsessively active. At work, she volunteered to lead the firm's non-profit efforts, namely, providing pro bono PR services to fledgling Black-owned businesses. When she wasn't working, she'd troll social media to repost something from Obama or the NAACP, or to chastise her friends who'd posted selfies without face masks at supposedly socially distanced brunches. As much as she wanted to attend the protests, Link convinced her to stay home. The risk was too great, and they were already so overwhelmed with the move and the pandemic. She agreed but made plans to attend a peaceful protest on the day of his flight and another one the following weekend.

The Black Lives Matter protests climaxed during the week of his move. The night before his flight to California, Uber and Lyft had announced they'd be suspending their services because of a newly instated eight p.m. curfew in New York, which was Mayor de Blasio's veiled attempt to trap and arrest protesters with bullshit cause. For several nights thereafter, de Blasio's army of riot police would block either exit of the city's bridges just before the clock struck eight, so that those marching peacefully across them would be in violation of his order. No one would be allowed to leave their homes till five in the morning, which worried Link because he had an early flight. He ordered a private car service, praying it'd show up on time.

Erica and Link didn't have goodbye sex on their last night together. They were too emotionally exhausted from the last three tumultuous months of the lockdown, the unknown effects of their nearing physical separation, and the uncertainty of their long-term future as husband and wife. Instead, she opted to cry to sleep in his apprehensive arms.

The next morning, his driver arrived promptly at four forty-five. Half asleep, Erica followed Link downstairs with his backpack on her small shoulder as he lugged the rest of his heavier baggage to the black town car—their doorman had been out sick. Link hugged her tightly for a good sixty seconds, going through the motions of a big farewell but expecting to feel more emotional. The onlooking driver eating a McDonald's breakfast sandwich made it awkward, and the lack of sleep further dulled his emotions. It wasn't until the plane was more than halfway across the country, after he'd watched the film *JoJo Rabbit* on the back of the seat in front of him, that he suddenly broke down from it all. He sobbed as quietly as possible behind the white bandana that covered half his face. His tears and snot soaked through the cloth, so much so he had to swap it for one of the disposable masks he'd packed as backups. Fortunately, Delta Airlines had cordoned off every other seat, so no one witnessed his emotional breakdown.

Link's grief has dissipated quickly. Now that he's settling into California living, he's feeling free and easy like a man on vacation. For once, he has room to breathe and think. Over the last few weeks, he's busied himself with buying a car—a new BMW X5—ordering and assembling new furniture and home décor; familiarizing himself with the healthy neighborhood eats; catching up with close friends and old college buddies who moved west before him; and braving the nearby hiking trails of varying difficulty and danger, concurrently facing his fear of potential encounters with rattlesnakes and mountain lions, however rare. He's also flourished in his new role at Pure. His culturally relevant creative ideas have helped the agency win two new clients! The cancellation of *Holy War*, the onslaught of the pandemic and his wife's abortion hasn't killed his inspiration after all.

Nor has he missed Erica much, despite how he comes across in the obligatory goodnight-love-you texts and semi-weekly miss-you-so-much FaceTimes. Thoughts of divorce and how to go about it have been incessant. He's been listening on repeat to "Break Your Heart" from *Rock Spectacle* by Barenaked Ladies, a favorite album in his youth, while

driving teary eyed in his new car. She hasn't suspected anything out of the ordinary, which, in his mind, only further
proves how out of sync they are. Their conversation has been
limited to the topics of missing each other and which bike
protest she's going to next, each of which has a color-themed
dress code to rationalize her excessive online shopping. "I
can't very well fight for justice when ride organizers are calling for orange and I have nothing orange in my closet!" She
hardly seems focused on the move anymore, which, he's hoping, means she's realizing that they're better off apart.

He decides to take a ride up the lovely Pacific Coast Highway. Cooler air is coming off the sea, blowing his hair every
which way. Mountains at varying distances offer a layered
landscape of beauty that looks fake seen through the eyes of
a longtime New Yorker who hardly left the city, apart from
business travel. These drives remind him why he moved—escaped—to Dreamland, California. He makes a right off the
exit to the highway and flies up the steep Temescal Canyon
Road.

At the top, he parks across the street from a sun-drenched
Palisades Charter High School. It has an all-American vibe
and features a sprawling football field and a professional-
sized swimming pool. Due to the pandemic, both are completely devoid of people, as is the rest of the campus. Link
tries to live his life without envy, but in gorgeous neighborhoods with perfect schools like this, where proof of happier

childhoods than he had are so prevalent, he gets a sharp pang in his sixpack, like someone stabbed him.

He would know the feeling. When he was seventeen, a group of classmates at Breakneck jumped him and stuck him with a pocketknife—just a flesh wound. He grabs his phone, headphones, bandana and water bottle, leaving his wallet and keys in the car—which boasts keyless entry—and heads toward the Temescal Canyon trailhead. The park is usually busier on weekday afternoons, what with all those working from home needing a brief reprieve from Zoom calls and furious typing. Today it's oddly empty save for an old woman doing a lap of power walking around the parking lot. The heat coming off the pavement is quite visible, which reminds Link how much hotter it is up here versus around his bungalow down by the beach.

The beginning of the trail is steep and zigzags all the way to the first of several peaks. The farther up he goes, the less shade there is to rest and cool off—odd because he's never had to stop so often on past hikes here. Everything is the same: red dirt trail; sporadic whiffs of animal shit carried in breeze otherwise scented with wildflowers; frequent lizards providing fast company as they sprint in and out of view; giant black and green snakes—no sighting of rattlesnakes yet—slithering across the well-trod path as if they didn't have a care in the world. The sun beats his face worse than those kids who jumped him back in the day.

There's no more wind, the air is dead, as is most of the water-starved vegetation that surrounds him. Foreboding cacti to his left and right have been defaced with various initials and hearts carved into them, likely by young lovers who are long broken up, the plants forever scarred and unsightly for naught. The cacti gloat at a parched Link as they quench their thirst with the water their bodies retained from the last rainfall more than three months ago. This throws him into a rage. His water bottle is already empty. He drank half of it and poured the rest on his fevered head just thirty seconds ago, but he's already thirsty and burning up again. His legs and lower intestines are trembling, the contents of the latter audibly moving about inside him. He feels like shitting and vomiting in tandem, and it's taking all his muscle strength to hold everything in. Controlling his bowel movements while walking proves challenging, but he knows he'll make it if he can get past the difficult part. It's either that or run off-trail into unmaintained foliage to defecate somewhat privately, but with that comes the risk of the possibly poisonous wildlife in the brush biting his balls. He must keep going.

He finds sad excuses for shade beneath the dead branches of leafless bushes, which do nothing to satiate his suffering as he practically crawls the rest of the way up, his head pounding worse than any migraine. Every twenty feet or so he must stop to rest, or he'll lose his shit—literally. No one has passed him in either direction. He lies on his back in the middle of the trail, the dirt and likely reptile shit mixing with his hair and sticking to his sweaty bare torso. Pulling out his phone, he considers calling 911, but there's no service. "Fuck you, Telco!" he screams.

An earlier text notification from Erica is on display. "New York just isn't New York without you, honeybun." He looks at the text, shoves the phone in his pocket and gazes up at the sky, taking labored breaths. A collection of misfit seemingly stagnant clouds resembles the shape of nothing. This would've gone so differently with his wife by his side. Erica would've remembered to carry extra bottles of water or convince him to save the hike for a cooler day. She's been his faithful partner for all these years. He's realizing that her devotion, his vows, the love they've fostered, is more important than procuring the family of his dreams. Even if that means not having children.

The revelation brings him to his feet, motivating him to put one foot in front of the other, right, left, right, left. He won't succumb to the overbearing sun, the bone-dry earth emitting visible heat, the nearby Joshua trees like *Beetlejuice* sculptures, the unseen famished mountain lions and paralyzing rattlesnakes. The sun keeps shining down on him, burning his forehead like the highest of fevers, but he keeps going, albeit at turtle-speed. Hiking over the red rocks is like bouldering versus just walking an uneven path. Rustling in the bushes convinces him that his prey is closing in, but he keeps going, his determination to finish the whole loop being a product of his military schooling. He makes it past the rocks and begins the steepest ascent to the tallest summit. What normally takes him ten minutes to hustle up the moderately difficult final peak takes thirty—plus a small deposit of diarrhea in his iridescent boxer briefs by Dark-White—but he makes it.

The slow descent feels longer than usual. Thankfully, the temperature is cooler the farther he drags himself. He gets to the bottom of the trail and heads to his car with immense relief, the love he has for his wife reinvigorated. On the way, he passes a single-person public restroom, but it's already in use. A father is screaming at his whining son while they wait to go next, which triggers Link's PTSD from boarding school. He casts back to when he and his classmates had to line up in the cafeteria in complete silence and those who spoke were met with physical punishment.

The mountainous peaks of Temescal Canyon loom behind a sun-beaten Link like one of the counselors at Breakneck who caught him trying to escape on a rainy night and beat him until he collapsed in a muddy puddle. These bad memories have materialized like the accidental shit in his pants, inescapable feelings of rejection and dismissal, of being unable to live up to the expectations of his father. After a final attempt to run away and a subsequent whipping, his emotional stamina withered away. He folded to Breakneck's rules and, ultimately, the will of his father. He even became one of the academy's night watchmen assigned to catching other students trying to flee. The relentless pressures of the academy's tough love program turned him from an unruly kid following his heart into the man he is today, living by the rules of a straight life, desperate for acceptance, to achieve the best job and optimal fitness through hard work and self-respect.

Back home he calls his honey Erica to fill her in on his death-defying hike.

"Honeybun, that is so scary, she says. "You're an experienced hiker… You know enough to check the weather. I mean, you could've died. Then what would I have done? I'm too young to be a widow."

"I know… I don't know, work has been insane, hon. I just rushed out to get in a hike between meetings and forgot to eat… I had to cancel the rest of my day today."

She exhales deeply. "Well yeah, you're severely dehydrated. Are you drinking water?"

"Don't worry, my sweet. I ate something, as hard as it was on my stomach. Been chugging water ever since. Got a Big Gulp cup filled with ice water right in front of me, sipping and thinking of you."

"Oh Link, I miss you so much! I wish I was there taking care of my honeybun. Can't wait till I'm moved out."

Achy all over and with a moderate headache, he adjusts his position on the couch, shifting from his back to his left side as her words comfort him in his sickly state. He's always been a big baby when he's unwell—like all men are, according to Erica.

Big Gulps from 7-Eleven are sentimental symbols of their love and marriage. As healthy as Erica and Link are, soda fountain Diet Coke is one of their very few guilty pleasures. After a lunch date in midtown Manhattan one sunny winter afternoon, he slid a diamond ring from Tiffany's onto the drinking straw of her Big Gulp. She didn't immediately notice it as they sat in the lobby of McCann, the ad agency where he worked then. Three sips later, looking up from her work phone, she yelped with glee. He never actually asked her to marry him, nor had he planned on proposing in the lobby of his office building, but he'd picked up the ring on the day before and it'd been burning a hole in his pocket ever since. She blurted out a yes loudly enough to ensure everyone around them took notice of her major life moment. Onlookers in business casual dress celebrated the proposal with a round of applause, some of whom followed her to the street to further congratulate her as she jumped hastily into an Uber, intent on making a meeting that she'd ultimately miss. Link stayed behind basking in exaggerated congratulations from strangers and a few of his co-workers.

He tells Erica he misses her, with sincerity for the first time in a while, and ends the call. Completely in love again but exhausted from the near-death hike, he turns on the TV, streams one of his beloved Marvel movies, jerks off to Scarlett Johansson in her superhero costume, and sleeps through the night.

Link used to always say no to drugs. Many of his friends, intimate and superficial alike, derange their senses with alcohol and party drugs to enjoy brief reprieves from everyday stresses like intense work weeks, trite arguments with significant others, etcetera. They need the weekend binge to achieve moments of mental quietude, to hear their souls, to understand their true selves rather than the unreliable, limiting thoughts of the human brain. For them, drugs catalyze their art, written, visual and otherwise. The short-term effects break through the mental walls they've been building up since childhood to protect themselves from various traumas. Sometimes their enlightenment lasts longer than the trip, say, after the indescribable journey of peyote or acid. In its purer form, cocaine can be a good truth serum and release their inhibitions. But Link used to always avoid drugs because he believed they'd inhibit his motivation to exercise, eat clean or pull an all-nighter at work.

Despite his historical position on the subject, and after having bragged about it as naively and self-righteously as the lyrics to "Xanny" by Billie Eilish, he's been smoking weed daily since moving to California. His friends back home consider his newly contradictory behavior quite hilarious. For him, it's a big change. On his cross-country flight, after mourning the end of a long, infamously hard but fortuitous life in New York, he decided to be more open-minded, to try whatever L.A. had to offer.

He loves taking cannabis by vaping it, specifically the brand Green Crack, which is sativa in its strongest form, ninety percent THC. Last week he smoked at a co-worker's birthday barbecue—outdoors, of course, given the pandemic. A blonde with big boobs and a flat ass was hitting on him hard. He almost kissed her but ultimately resisted the temptation, determined to make it work with Erica.

His dramatic shift in mindset can be attributed to the present insanity of life on earth: his marriage troubles; the mentally debilitating pandemic; his naive feelings of guilt and helplessness as a straight white man watching the hopeless news of cops killing Black people and getting away with it like they had in the fifties; the country polarized by Trump's presidency; the public's disillusionment about Markus which cost Link the *Holy War* project—not to mention what happened to Ella...

A stoned Link chuckles compulsively every time his friend Tony, who's teaching a sound bath class, rolls a small mallet around a giant crystal bowl and hums a little ditty. Tony, a former creative director at Pure, quit the agency, the advertising industry and New York in one fell swoop after a nervous breakdown due to burning the candle at both ends of work and play, and escaped to California. Three years later, here he is, teaching ancient-Indian physical and spiritual practices in the guest house of a mini mansion in Brentwood that he owns with his hot older wife. Link has swapped three lifting days at home for yoga at Tony's, restoring his sixpack, gaining leaner muscles and a sharper mind. Yoga has also helped calm his worries about Erica's arrival in a few weeks. As excited as he is about seeing her, residuals of anxiety and confusion remain. It's as though the last three months alone have erased their whole relationship, and they'll be meeting as strangers with all the thrills and uncertainty that come with it.

As hard as he's fallen for vinyasa and meditative yoga, he's unable to take the sound bath seriously. All the others in class are tight-bod models or older white women from the neighborhood—Tony has always preferred the vintage ladies. The woman lying next to Link is farting silently, acting as if he can't tell where the smell is coming from. Maybe she doesn't realize it's happening. He tries to focus on himself, but the THC chewable he and Tony took before class is making it difficult.

The sound bath ends with the sweet song of Tony's gentle gong. The giggles from Link's high have calmed, permitting a quietness of his soul to flow in. An overwhelming sense of joy and peace rush from his feet to his head like the best kind of orgasm, the one from making love. He rises slowly to his feet with the rest of the class. Tony whispers sugary goodbyes to the ladies, bear-hugging each of them as they walk out. They mosey down the freshly paved driveway, chatting softly. Once they're all gone, Link embraces Tony just the same.

"Thanks, man," Link says, feeling invigorated, thrilled to be alive and to have his honeybun Erica in his arms soon.

"Love you, dude," Tony replies.

Robin breezes through the doors that lead to the arrivals pickup area in Terminal 2 at LAX, where Link is waiting eagerly. After spending the last few globally tragic months alone, he's desperate for a familiar face, and she doesn't disappoint. Her flowing black summer dress is patterned in red flowers. Her arms swing at her sides as she reaches him with an ear-to-ear smile and a big hug at the ready.

"Robin! It's been too long."

"Facts. *So* good to see you and *finally* get a moment away from New York."

"Stoked to have another friend around. My much-needed alone time has lost its allure, plus everyone is so flaky with plans here. Now I'm just bored and lonely... thank God Erica will be here soon."

They stroll to his car a few feet away, its hazard lights aggravating the faint awkwardness in their exchange. All their fond memories and uninhibited texts, his FaceTimes with a wine-drenched Robin, have proven incomparable to a face-to-face. He struggles with her overstuffed Louis luggage, feeling somewhat anxious about having Pure Creative's CEO as a guest in his home. But he understands her concerns about staying in a hotel or Airbnb during the pandemic, so he tries to relax. Remembering to lift with his legs, he tosses the

luggage into the trunk with ease and an exhalation of gratitude. He's been desperate for this pause from the tiring sixty-
hour workweeks, the waning joy of alone time, the monotony
of seventy-two-and-sunny L.A. living, however beautiful his
nightly hikes and contemplative interludes with Tony have
been.

Robin's jovial disposition is a stark cry from the state she
was in after the *Holy War* project had been canceled. She'd
never broken her image of grace and authority before that
Friday. After announcing to the agency that they'd lost not
one but two major pieces of business that afternoon, she just
lost it. In one blunt breakup email, the *Holy War* project and
the separate rebranding work they'd been doing for Telco had
gone down the drain. Despite the latter project having no re-
lation to Markus, Pure had been too close to his team for
Telco's conservative chief marketing officer's liking. The
CMO decided to drop Pure entirely, going so far as to state
in writing that they'd been in breach of contract for failing to
manage the talent properly, which thereby damaged Telco's
"stellar reputation."

As Robin continued her speech to the agency, Link cast
back to everything they'd all suffered through to make their
dream in TV a reality: his team's cocaethylene-fueled binges
to perfect the work—only 5-hour Energy shots for him—and
the subsequent hangovers at client meetings; shameless infi-
delities when stuck in different zip codes than their spouses
for extended periods of time; group weight gain from donuts

and pizzas—excluding the very thin Ella, of course—to alleviate the stress of round-the-clock office hours and limited time for the gym; fights with lovers over late workdays and lost date nights. Robin's crying over their losses was almost as unsettling for Link as watching his sick mother moaning in agony.

"I want you all to know...," she sniffled, "how much I admire and respect you all, especially you, Link—and of course Ella and Brandon who aren't here with us. You're all so amazing, with kind souls and great talent that can't be publicized because of Markus's despicable actions. Sure, it's also cutting into our target for the year by several million, but I know—not think, *know*—that we'll reach it if we stick together."

As tears of exhaustion and defeat glazed the front of Link's eyes, the rest of the agency clapped with exaggeration, chanting, "We love you! We love you! We love you!"

He clapped in solidarity but with an unmentioned pit in his stomach for the missing members of the *Holy War* crew. Ella had just been arrested after being caught hiding out in Connecticut with her dead brother's best friend, Clay—luckily the major papers covering her trial, which is nearing closing remarks, have been predicting a hung jury. Brandon was still on extended leave to recover from the attack at the hotel, and he wouldn't be back to working remotely during the pandemic anytime soon, let alone in person whenever Pure's offices reopened post distribution of a vaccine. Not that Link or anyone else blamed him after what he'd been through. Robin hardly mentioned either of them in her speech to the agency. Pure's legal team had ordered her to give vague statements to the staff and press about their absences, what with the highly publicized criminal case against Ella and the unsolved sexual assault on Brandon—touchy subjects in the workplace.

At Link's bungalow, Robin is unpacking her suitcases, one of which holds bottles and jars of vitamins and supplements. She's carrying on about her self-diagnosed immunity to coronavirus as a result of her vegan diet, religious yoga routine, excess intake of natural anti-inflammatories, anti-aging remedies, immunity boosters and, most notably, "the end-all-be-all" supplement of Indigenous origin called lomatium. Used by many tribes to treat various infections, especially those affecting the lungs, she believes the lomatium root is a shoo-in for combatting COVID-19. She boasts of its benefits while ingesting about fifty different capsules over the course of fifteen minutes. "Fair warning, when you first start taking it, you may develop a rash, but it goes away."

Skeptical as he may be, Link can't argue with her statuesque physique, glowing skin and relaxing charisma. As a Black woman living through the tragic present, her glowing mood inspires him. He pops a couple ginseng and spirulina pills when she offers them after explaining their naturally energizing benefits.

"Send me a link to buy the lomatium," he says, knowing the allure of her sales pitch for ingesting a surplus of supplements will probably fade as soon as she's gone. He has his own methods for optimizing his health.

He glazes over current events to gauge her position on everything going on in the world, bragging about his wife's activism and gently inquiring about Robin's take on the protests. She admits she hasn't attended a single march in New York but recounts a road trip she took to a cousin's in Trump Country, when she and her boyfriend at the time were pulled over by police without cause other than being Black and driving after hours with out-of-state plates. She and her ex gave overly polite replies and kept their hands where the cop could see them.

Link listens intently, filled with empathy and guilt. Guiltily, compulsively, he thinks of how lucky and safe he is as a straight white man. He'll never suffer like that. He thinks of his wife and all the other "allies" of Blacks marching in protest for equal rights back in New York, in other major cities in the U.S. and around the world. Robin marches every day of her life, as a Black woman in the American workforce. He knows he'll never fully understand what she goes through or how much it hurts.

They eventually leave to grab takeout from a vegan Thai spot on Lincoln and bring it back to the pool in his complex. Technically, only residents are allowed in the pool area due to pandemic restrictions, but no one says anything. Link takes a pic of Robin lounging on a sun chair and shares it on social media with the caption "L.A. rays with @PureRobin." He won't admit it, but part of him does so just to show he has Black friends.

The next morning he's awakened by the sound of Robin's heavy, sexual breathing coming from the living room. From the TV playing at low volume, the voice of the yoga instructor directing Robin's expert poses quickly corrects Link's dirty-minded assumption. He ventures into the living room, interrupting her Zen.

"Morning! Sorry, did I wake you?" she asks.

"Not at all. Did you hear my snoring? Erica has to wear earplugs."

"Didn't hear a thing," she says, offering him a juice that she made with the expiring veggies in his fridge. "I passed right out as soon as my head hit the pillow, but I woke up *so* early. Still on New York time."

"Hope the guest room was comfortable for you? You're the first person to stay in it."

"Perfect, my friend, thank you."

"Should we hike today? I've only done Los Leones and Temescal, but I've been wanting to try this other trail called Rustic Canyon."

"Def. I'm in dire need of Mother Nature."

As overworked as he's been, he recognizes how rare it is to have such a close connection to the CEO. His tenure at the agency, the trust he's fostered over the years, he has to remind himself how good he has it. The casual job searching when he's stressed out and imagining bigger and better paying opportunities brand-side isn't the cure for his unease. Work is work, so why switch positions during these unpredictable times? Someone newly hired at his level will be the first one on the chopping block if sales decline. He should stay put. The same goes for his marriage. The incessant ambition to live his best life in all aspects may be to his detriment. There's nowhere to go. Besides, he has everything he needs right now.

Robin declines the joint he offers before the hike.

"I don't know why, but THC and nature have really given me a new perspective on life," he says.

"Not for me, but go ahead," she says without judgment. "All wine is fine for me, but the rest... I'm completely clueless and uninterested. It was only after I fired Axel that I learned about his drug problems. One of our beauty clients told me on a call that she'd ran into Axel, *my chief creative officer,* all sweaty and nervous in Williamsburg at eight in the morning like some crackhead. I reminded her he's no longer with us."

"You didn't know about the drugs? I thought everyone knew! He was always running around the office with that twitchy face... and I still can't get over that time he flew back drunk from the pitch in Chicago and got caught smoking in the airplane bathroom."

Her eyes widen. "I did not know this," she says, shaking her head.

"That was over a year ago."

"Wow. Well, lucky for him I didn't know because he'd have been gone a lot sooner."

"I knew he was shit from the start, but I wanted to give him the benefit of the doubt."

"Mm-hmm," Robin interjects with a smirk on her face.

"He ended up digging his own grave, anyway. I just think he had absolutely no creative point of view... know what I mean? Aside from his cultish approach to inspire the agency, he never contributed anything to the work during creative reviews. It was only ever silence during meetings other than saying, 'Looks good.'"

"Tell us how you really feel!" She dips her head back laughing, her skin glistening with perspiration.

The Lululemon yoga pants fit her too perfectly and cause a stir in his boxer briefs. It's been quite a while, and wanting her has come up once or twice, but he'll never act on it. They'll never be closer than they are this morning.

On the drive to the mountain, Link is regretting having offered Robin the car keys. He knows she has her license and drives rentals during business trips, but this is the first time he's driven with her. Giving new meaning to riding everyone's ass, she tails drivers so closely that she's had three very close calls earmarked by his car's unnerving beeping warning of a potential collision, and she's missed their turn twice. His phone signal is weakening in the hills, so Google Maps is taking longer to re-route every time she goes the wrong way. He pulls a hit from the weed pen and relaxes. She opens all the car windows as they drive further into Brentwood, where all the houses are beautiful but dramatically varying in style.

He absorbs the view in amazement, adding owning one of these special homes in a luxurious neighborhood to his five-year goals. There's a magnificent modern masterpiece sitting on the corner of the dead-end street that Google Maps shows as an alternate entrance to Rustic Canyon Trail since she already led them away from the main one. The house is rumored to be Pharrell's, at least that's what Tony's yoga ladies told Link when he mentioned plans to hike around here. They park in front of a white antebellum-style mansion with a wraparound balcony, as if they were in the South rather than some bourgeois L.A. neighborhood. The red and yellow flowers woven through the tall black gate surrounding the home evoke sentiments of New Orleans.

Down the dead-end street they walk, then onward to the trail. Most trails in the Pacific Palisades are red and sandy, but not this one. It's just an old road overgrown with weeds that sprout greedily from the cracks in the pavement, the result of seemingly a half-century's worth of harsh sunlight and rare rains. As far as they can see, graffiti is tattooed on nearly every inch of the dilapidated road. Much of it is recent: "Black Lives Matter," "Justice for Breonna Taylor," "#Fuck-Trump."

They follow the long, winding street, which wraps around the curvy canyon wall to their right. Breathtaking mansions of all shapes and sizes that were visible a half hour ago when they entered the trail have shrunk and will soon disappear. Link finds it odd that they've only passed one other hiker for nearly an hour. She was skinny, tall and naturally blond, and had Scandinavian features. Saturday is usually prime hiking time, when the trails are packed with people opting to defy the state's temporary rule on wearing face masks outside. Today it's like a creepy ghost town. He's also a bit high, so the weed may be making him paranoid. They reach the top of the hill, the descent of which drops sharply and is darker. The opposing wall of the canyon completely blocks the wonderful, watchful sun.

"Seems a bit eerie," he says.

"I'm intrigued... Man, feels so good to be out here."

"Yeah," he says, looking around. "But what's with these telephone poles? They go on forever like this is some old residential street. Feels like we're in another time."

"Get it together, pothead."

He cracks up. "You're right. Let's keep going. There was a landmark named Murphy's Ranch near here on Google Maps. Pretty sure they use these roads for horse riding or something."

"Yeah... Sorry, one sec. I just got a signal and need to respond to a few work emails."

"Our jobs are never done, especially yours."

"The trials of being ballers."

They descend to the floor of the canyon, approaching a tunnel made of thick trees. Crooked branches with murky-pond-colored leaves reach for one another from either side of the dark street to form a foreboding arch over the road before them.

"Okay, signal's gone again," she says, a little irritated. "My stomach is about to pop off from my morning vitamins... Also, have you noticed all the graffiti is dated and faded now? I just saw my birth year written in red spray paint."

"We can turn back if you don't feel comfortable."

"I'm good for a bit longer." She rubs her nearly concave sixpack and continues walking.

He follows her into the dark, a tad resentful. Up the road is a turnoff with a brick pillar at the corner. "That must've been someone's driveway," he says, always fascinated by artifacts of the past.

Daring each other to check it out, they head up. What they find is the brick foundation of what must've once been the impressive home of the affluent owners of the canyon. Heading back down, they turn onto the main road, where they eventually find a couple other driveways that lead to weedy foundations and the ruins of raised gardens. Far above their heads the sky is a glorious blue, but down where they're exploring the architectural skeletons of some long-gone town, the light has dimmed tremendously, like the sun is setting in early afternoon.

Before them is a boarded-up building shaped like a steeple. Painted matte black, it's smothered in every language and color of graffiti. Silver swastikas painted over "Black Lives Matter!" and "MAGA" written over "Not My President." These provocative words are next to the question of a lifetime: "Sally, Will You Marry Me?" The Graffiti Church—as Robin has just named it—evokes messages of opposing sides, broadcasting the ugliness of racism, the endless fight against hate. The statements are often misspelled in browning orange spray paint, a tacky silver or alarming yellow.

"What the hell is this place?" she asks, snapping selfies in front of the Graffiti Church, pointing at it with a WTF look on her dewy face. "Damn, it won't post. No service again."

"Yeah, same for me. I've been trying to look this place up. Now I'm really curious."

"This was a Nazi camp," says the blond hiker from earlier.

Robin gasps. Link yelps like his dead dog—his and Erica's Miley kicked the bucket shortly after he moved west. The blond hiker seems to have appeared out of thin air. It's the same woman they ran into a while back, only now she's with a guy who's also blond, taller than she is, and with comparable Scandinavian features. She's dressed in a black-and-white striped T-shirt, black leggings and white tennis shoes. He's in a navy blue polo, khaki shorts and boat shoes. With Link and

Robin's heads in their phones, they hadn't noticed them walking up.

"Man, y'all scared the hell out of me! Shit!" She fans herself, taking deep breaths.

"Same, sweating over here," Link says.

"Oh, excuse us!" the woman says.

"Yes, sincerest apologies," the man says.

"So sorry," the woman apologizes again. "I just overheard your conversation and thought I'd share my knowledge of this place. You know, Murphy's Ranch? Oh, I'm Winnie by the way, and this is my husband, Norm."

"Pleasure," he chimes in, as if on cue. Boldly extending a pale hand as if being overly polite at the age of twentysomething and named Norm is at all *normal*, he reminds Link of theater actors trained to emote via exaggerated gestures of the body.

Link accepts his handshake while looking to his right, distracted by the heaping offering of rusty cans of spray paint piled high before the front of the Graffiti Church. Littered everywhere, they're from seemingly every decade of the last fifty years, that is, based on the labels of new and old design—he studied product design in college. On this defaced building, Americans of varying decency speak their ugly truths. Greeting these blond oddballs who have *American Psycho* smiles and virtually transparent blue eyes, he's suddenly overwhelmed by the angry history of this place.

"Well, it wasn't a Nazi camp *per se*... but kind of like a compound," Norm says.

"More like a sanctuary?" Winnie adds.

"Yeah! Exactly!" Norm says. "Built and owned by the Stephens family. They were certain that Germany would win the war, and that when the Third Reich arrived in the U.S., they'd need a place to lie low while the dust settled."

Robin is in a downward dog pose stretching out her calves and feet. The empty expression on her face between her sculpted legs implies she isn't very interested in the history of white supremacists. Norm continues explaining that the Stephens's were rich but built this place with practicality in mind. They raised Murphy's Ranch to be self-sustaining for long periods of time, replete with a bomb shelter, water and fuel tanks, and several residential buildings and bunkers. They also planned to build a mansion fit for a world leader, a "Nazi White House," but the idea hadn't gone further than architectural drawings. It was only after they'd sold the land to a woman named Jessie M. Murphy in 1933 that it received its permanent moniker, Murphy's Ranch.

Link thinks of taking a selfie by the Graffiti Church and posting it on Instagram with his location tagged and the caption reading, "Stumbled upon an old Nazi camp hiking today. Just another day in L.A.," but he's worried Robin will find it tone-deaf.

"Nice to meet ya. Let's get out of here," she says.

Links takes the hint. "Yeah, man, thanks."

"It was so nice meeting you two," Winnie says in the tone of a sorority girl complimenting a chubby freshman on his new ill-fitting jeans.

"Pleasure," Norm says.

"Okay!" Robin turns to Link, smiling ear to ear with wide eyes.

He nods and begins walking away with her. The blond couple stand in place holding hands, seeing them off like parents watching their kids board a school bus for the first time. They're only a couple yards away when Norm calls them back.

"Say, we meant to ask, can you throw us a few bucks?"

"You know," Winnie adds, her eyes narrowing, "for the history lesson."

"That's right, my sweet." Norm's friendly smile mutates into Joker's grin.

"Sorry, dude," Link says firmly. "Wallet's in the car."

"Come on, let's go," Robin insists.

Link gives Norm a departing shrug, then suddenly finds himself face down on the ground. It takes a few seconds to realize he's been hit in the back of the head with one of the spray paint cans. It skips a few feet past him, eventually settling in front of Robin.

"Motherfucker!" she hollers, preparing to charge at Norm, but Winnie pushes her from behind and she comes crashing down beside Link.

Winnie's high-pitched cackle is giving him Harley Quinn vibes. From where he lies in an awkward position, he spots rings of black around the cuffs of Norm's stained khakis. He looks up to Winnie with her psycho killer eyes and her hair greasy near the scalp. How did he miss how dirty and desperate they look—and perhaps homeless? The clothes, the probably false names, the friendliness, it's all been a front. He decides to blame his poor judgment on the cannabis.

Norm is kicking Link in the ribs, but his repeated blows aren't doing much damage because his symptoms of withdrawal from opioids are making him weak—Link's muscular chest may have something to do with it, too. The blood trickling down Link's face and threatening to get in his eyes is more concerning. Regardless, Norm's kicking paired with a hit to the head is enough to keep him down. Winnie mounts a dazed Robin, whose forehead is scratched from when she went down face first.

"You nasty cunt! I know you got some titty money. Give it here before I bash your head in." She fingers around inside Robin's bra, eventually giving up. "Fuck!"

"What?" Norm asks breathlessly.

"This Black bitch ain't got shit!"

"Take her Apple Watch!"

Link hears another smack, but it's less sharp this time. It sounds more like a thump. Winnie falls to the ground, a welt forming on her right cheek at warp speed. Robin is standing over her, breathing audibly, a can of spray paint in her right hand. Her eyes are filled with equal parts fury, fear and sadness. She looks up at Norm bolting down the crumbling street.

"You better run, motherfucker! Oh, oh, you don't want your girl?" She spits on an unconscious Winnie. "Can you walk?" she asks Link as softly as possible with her blood still boiling, while helping him to his feet.

He shakes his head and takes a few deep breaths. Robin's sweaty, scratched face comes into focus. "Yeah, I think so."

"It's best you stay awake in case of a concussion. Let's start back while I try for service."

"Are you okay?"

With downcast eyes, trembling lips and her eyes tearing up, she says, "I just need a minute."

"What about her?" he asks noncommittally, looking down at Winnie.

"Fuck this crackhead."

With Robin cutting her visit short to spend the rest of her time in California at a second cousin's desert cabin outside Palm Springs, Link feels more alone than ever. His father called him on the anniversary of his mother's death—the only time of year they chat besides the obligatory end-of-year holidays— but he didn't pick up. After Link had been discharged from the hospital with eleven stitches and mildly bruised ribs, Robin stuck around till his concussion healed, but that was almost a week ago. He's beyond desperate for Erica's arrival.

It's only a few hours away, but it feels like an eternity. Giving his statement to the police as the EMT prepped him for transfer to the hospital felt just as long.

Waking from a weed-induced afternoon snooze, he replays the attempted mugging in his mind. He's never been more terrified or alive than he was in that canyon. The only thing close to it was the time his father caught him stealing cash from his wallet, after which he sent him to his first boarding school.

Thrills aside, Link feels terrible for Robin. He can only imagine how much she's suffering. This beautiful, powerful woman from a humble neighborhood in Queens who's risen to the top of her field—she was just named number one in *AdAge's* Top 50—subjected to such pure hate. He isn't surprised that the news of what happened is going viral: "Ad Exec Attacked in Nazi Camp Ruins." At least the free press will do wonders for her career, and for redeeming Pure Creative after the whole Markus debacle. Soon the police will catch Norm and Winnie and this whole thing will really pop—although the cops are saying it'll be difficult because the pair gave fake names. Link will later learn that Norm and Winnie were inspired by the names of the original owners of Murphy's Ranch: Norman and Winona Stephens—the Stephens's!

As Erica waves her arm in the air, the giant graphic of a Black fist on the front of her oversized T-shirt seems to be waving too. She wears her hair pulled back and is dressed in fitted windbreaker pants. Link thinks of the legendary Fly Girls from *In Living Color*. He's aching for sex.

"Honey bunny!" she squeals, jumping into his arms, her right hand clutching the back of his head.

"Ow! Careful, hon."

"Oh, your stitches! My lord, oh my gosh," she says, kissing his forehead, nose and lips.

With an erection growing in his sweatpants, he rushes her into the car, afraid of being arrested for public indecency. Speeding home in minutes, he gets her in bed just as quickly.

A minute ago, Erica was in his arms. Now she's in the hospital, fighting for her life. It was only after she'd gotten sick from coronavirus while traveling to L.A. that Link learned of her childhood asthma and bouts of pneumonia—she's always wanted to be perceived as a picture of health, even to her honeybun. He envisions her waving hello at the airport as he waves goodbye to her through the Tyvek hazmat suit the hospital is making him wear. She waves back with one hand, holding his gloved hand with the other, the up and down motion of the ventilator attached to her face a metal alien seeming to be sucking the life out of her.

The virus takes fewer than three days from the onset of her symptoms to the time it kills her. Her parents are still in the air when it happens, on their way from New York. It's just Link holding her lifeless hand as a disaffected nurse

unplugs the machines. Erica is dead, and he's alone again...
possibly forever.

Home after the hospital and a strained dinner at Soho Warehouse with Erica's drunken, inconsolable parents causing
quite the scene, Link stands in the bathroom of his bungalow
naked and dripping water, having forgotten to grab a towel
before showering. He envisions a lonely future of extended
bereavement leave from work, during which he'll oversleep,
lie around, smoke weed, and order every meal from Chick-fil-
A and In-N-Out. His sixpack will go missing as a result of his
slacking off his daily workout routine. Other thoughts and
feelings bounce around his brain, ranging from those of grief
over Erica and his mother, and to those of logistics. What
about the funeral? Should he have it here or send her back
East like her parents asked? How much will he inherit from
her life insurance? He didn't give her enough love. She
shouldn't have had to fight so hard for their marriage. He
should've *really* loved her. Will he ever forgive himself?

He exits the bathroom, airing dry, his balls shriveling from
the air conditioning. Lying on his back on the bed, he lays a
hand over his genitals and begins rubbing. He fantasizes
about Robin fighting those assholes and making love to him
afterward. The stunning face of his thirty-five-year-old
mother—the same age as Link now—becomes Erica's as he
imagines her going down on him. "It's okay, baby. It's okay,"
he whispers. The fantasy comes with mixed emotions of love

and sadness, so he pushes her off. He visualizes Robin bending over and taking orders from the yoga instructor. "Like a good girl, a real good girl... My girl!" A rush of blood washes over him as he ejaculates more semen than ever before.

The orgasm ends. He opens his eyes to the tidy room, sees the come in his trembling hand. The smell of a fart he released when he ejaculated lingers. He takes a deep breath, breaking down as he exhales. Soap opera sobbing, he covers his face in his hands, getting some of the goo in his eyes. He thinks of Erica's grieving parents, the uncertainty of the nearing election to replace the man he holds responsible for her death, and the possibility of being infected too despite having tested negative twice. He's disgusted with himself for neglecting Erica and objectifying Robin. He's worried about someone stealing his job while he's off work, and about whether his own father will blame him for Erica's death.

Wiping his burning eyes, Link pushes himself up and off the bed. He stands before a full-length mirror, examining his convulsing tight torso, his reddening face. The crying slows as he dries and dresses. In utter despair, and with an unacknowledged sense of freedom, he opens the sliding glass door to the backyard and steps outside. The eternal California sun comforts him.

This portable is free when

you support White Lexi.

HOLY WAR IS NO MORE
but White Lexi is here to stay.
Rest in peace, Markus...
Live in conflict, Elizabeth-*er*-
White Lexi-*er*-Liz Arnold!
Purchase your very own ITNA
television today and get a
FREE portable on us!*
All profits will go toward
funding her next adventure
—in prison!

ITNA
itnapress.com

*False advertising

About the Author

CHRISTOPHER STODDARD is the author of three other novels: *At Night Only* (ITNA, 2018), *Limiters* (ITNA, 2014), and *White, Christian* (Spuyten Duyvil, 2010). His most recent book, *At Night Only*, was praised by PEN award-winning author Edmund White, and was a staff pick in *The Paris Review*. For more than a decade, he worked at various ad agencies in New York City. He lives in L.A.

Books by ITNA

Urban Gothic: The Complete Stories
Bruce Benderson

Crashing Cathedrals: Edmund White by the Book
Tom Cardamone

The Beads
David McConnell

Tiny Fish that Only Want to Kiss
Gary Indiana

Everything Must Go
Lauren John Joseph

At Night Only
Christopher Stoddard

CPSIA information can be obtained
at www.ICGtesting.com
Printed in the USA
LVHW051952300422
717402LV00004B/8